"Why were you at Tracy's?" Alyssa asked suddenly. "I didn't think marshals got involved with local crimes."

"They don't. This isn't a local crime. I think we may be dealing with a serial killer. One who targets women in law enforcement."

"Micah, I hope you're wrong. The thought of a serial killer in our small community is beyond terrifying." Her brow crinkled. "But why did he attack me? I'm not in law enforcement."

"I was hoping you'd be able to remember that. I believe you might have seen something or witnessed something that put you in danger."

She chewed her lower lip. He found the action distracting and withdrew his gaze, choosing to stare out the window.

"I don't remember anything about the crime scene or the killer," she finally admitted. "But I do wonder if he'll come after me again."

He wondered the same thing. "I won't abandon you. I plan to stick to you like glue until he's caught."

Dana R. Lynn grew up in Illinois. She met her husband at a wedding and told her parents she'd met the man she was going to marry. Nineteen months later, they were married. Today, they live in rural Pennsylvania with their three children and a variety of animals. In addition to writing, she works as a teacher for the deaf and hard of hearing and is active in her church.

Books by Dana R. Lynn

Love Inspired Suspense

Amish Country Justice

Plain Target
Plain Retribution
Amish Christmas Abduction
Amish Country Ambush
Amish Christmas Emergency
Guarding the Amish Midwife
Hidden in Amish Country
Plain Refuge
Deadly Amish Reunion
Amish Country Threats
Covert Amish Investigation
Amish Christmas Escape
Amish Cradle Conspiracy
Her Secret Amish Past
Crime Scene Witness

Visit the Author Profile page at LoveInspired.com for more titles.

CRIME SCENE WITNESS

DANA R. LYNN

LOVE INSPIRED SUSPENSE
INSPIRATIONAL ROMANCE

LOVE INSPIRED® SUSPENSE
INSPIRATIONAL ROMANCE

ISBN-13: 978-1-335-58769-5

Recycling programs
for this product may
not exist in your area.

Crime Scene Witness

This is a work of fiction. Names, characters, places and incidents are either the
product of the author's imagination or are used fictitiously. Any resemblance
to actual persons, living or dead, businesses, companies, events or locales is
entirely coincidental.

For questions and comments about the quality of this book, please contact us
at CustomerService@Harlequin.com.

Love Inspired
22 Adelaide St. West, 41st Floor
Toronto, Ontario M5H 4E3, Canada
www.LoveInspired.com

Printed in U.S.A.

Be careful for nothing; but in every thing by prayer and supplication with thanksgiving let your requests be made known unto God. And the peace of God, which passeth all understanding, shall keep your hearts and minds through Christ Jesus.
—*Philippians* 4:6-7

For my children.
It has been a blessing to watch you grow into adults.

All my love,

Mom

ONE

"Come on, Tracy. Text me back."

Alyssa Page drummed her short, sporty-length pink-and-silver acrylic nails against the wooden tabletop and stared at her phone, as if she could force her friend to answer by sheer will. The man at the booth in front of her turned and glared at her.

"Do you mind?"

She stilled her fingers. Her cheeks grew warm. "Sorry."

She discreetly combed her fingers through her long brown hair, her movements camouflaging the magnetic processor on the side of her head. She touched the one on the alternate side to ensure it was hidden, as well. Although she'd worn dual cochlear implants since she was eighteen months old, recent events had stirred her old feelings of self-consciousness to life.

It was all Teddy's fault.

She took a swallow of water, washing away the bitter taste his name caused. When Lissa met Teddy three years ago, she'd thought she'd finally met someone who saw beyond her past mistakes. She'd had to drop out of college at twenty when she'd become pregnant. She'd expected her boyfriend to propose when she told him he was going to be a father, but he had dumped her before she'd finished telling him about the baby. Her mother had been mortified. Lissa's stepfather was an up-and-coming politician, and having a pregnant stepdaughter hanging around wouldn't look good, so Lissa was on her own.

Lissa had no degree, and little by way of training. It was a struggle surviving and keeping food in her baby's stomach. She'd seen an ad for a crime scene cleaner and had applied in desperation. She needed to support herself and her baby, and the position didn't require more than a high school diploma.

She and Shelby had been on their own until Teddy had asked her out. He had seemed like the perfect boyfriend, and she'd begun to dream of having someone in her life. Until she'd met his parents, who had clearly not approved. The next week, Teddy had broken up with her. He wanted freedom. He couldn't have that if he was, as he'd spat at her, "shackled" to someone else's kid and a wife who was deaf.

His words had slammed into her like a jackhammer. She could see his mother's sneer stamped on his face. Before then, Shelby's existence hadn't bothered him. Nor had he ever minded that she was deaf. After all, she'd always been deaf. It wasn't something new. It usually didn't interfere with communication. When her implants were turned on, she heard a wide variety of noises. Although she missed some higher-pitched sounds, she caught most speech. But not all. Without her implants, she heard nothing.

Blinking the emotion from her eyes, she faced the empty chair across from her.

Her best friend, rookie officer Tracy Huber, hadn't shown for the lunch they'd been planning for the past eight days. No call. No text. Nothing. This wasn't like her. Since the day they'd met at the beginning of sixth grade, the other girl had always been the most reliable person Lissa had ever met. Even fifteen years later, it was still true.

Plus, Tracy never missed out on a birthday lunch. Every year, they took each other out for their birthdays. Tracy had turned twenty-six last week, on April 21, but this was the first day they'd both had free to get together.

No, something was wrong. Maybe Tracy was sick again. If that was the case, hopefully she'd go see a doctor before her yearly spring encounter with bronchitis developed into walking pneumonia again. It caught her off guard every April like clockwork.

Lissa cast one last glance at the time on her cell phone. She'd used up most of the time she had before she needed to collect Shelby from the babysitter and had yet to eat. Sighing, she took one last long swallow of her raspberry iced tea and rose from her seat. She'd drop by Tracy's house and check on her after she picked up Shelby.

Lissa dropped her cell phone into her purse and hurried out of the small coffee shop and café. It was starting to drizzle. Great. She lengthened her stride, intent on getting to her car before the skies opened up and it started to pour. Rain was in the forecast off and on for the next two days. Of course, she'd left her umbrella at home, sitting on the shelf where she set her purse each evening.

The rain started to fall harder. Lissa dashed to her car, sliding into her seat two seconds before the deluge struck.

She slammed the door closed, then checked her messages once more. Nothing. She couldn't shake the sense that something was wrong. She tried Tracy's number again. It went to voice mail. She hung up before it beeped for her to leave a message. Tracy would know her number if she saw it.

Her cell phone vibrated. She snatched up the phone, eagerly eyeing the display. Her brief spurt of excitement deflated like a popped balloon. It was only work calling. Sutter Springs Biohazard Cleaning. Lissa bit back a groan. It was a good job, she reminded herself. It paid the bills. And she needed the insurance.

Still, there was a price to pay for the work she did. Crime scenes were not for the faint of heart.

Punching the button, she answered the call.

"Hello."

"Lissa? It's Evan." Her boss, Evan Finch. He always identified himself, which was good. Sometimes she didn't recognize voices over the phone. "We have a bad one. SSPD. I know you're supposed to be off today, but I need you on this one. Gage is already on the way."

Sutter Springs Police Department. She knew what that meant. A murder scene, or at least a very bloody crime scene. Her gut knotted. Some days she hated her job.

"I understand. I can do it. I'll call my babysitter and

tell her I'll be late getting my daughter. Give me a second." She could always use the extra cash.

Sutter Springs, Ohio, was on the edge of Berlin County, about two hours northeast of Columbus. It wasn't a huge town, only about 50,000 people, but it was a booming Amish tourist attraction.

Lissa pressed her right foot down on the brake pedal and pushed the ignition button. Her phone connected, transferring the call to the car speaker. She opened the maps on her phone. She always used the GPS to locate the most efficient route to crime scenes.

"Okay, Evan. I have my map ready. Let me have the address." Her fingers hovered over her phone, ready to type.

He rattled off the address. Her hand froze and her blood turned to ice.

"Evan, check that address. I'm sure it's wrong."

Please God. Let it be wrong.

He repeated it. "That's the address they sent. Is it a problem?"

She couldn't respond. She hung up without thinking, pressing her foot down on the gas.

She didn't need to plug it into her GPS. She knew the address well. Tracy had lived in that house all her life, even after her father had remarried and moved across the country. When had she talked to Tracy last?

Yesterday. They'd confirmed their plans. Had anything been bothering Tracy? She wracked her brains but couldn't think of anything. Her friend hadn't been dating anyone, and she was focused on her career and repairing her relationship with her father.

The rain slowed, then stopped completely. Lissa took

advantage of the improved visibility and sped up, praying the entire drive that it was a mistake.

Arriving at Tracy's house, Lissa slowed down, eyeing the mass of police cruisers and crime scene unit
vehicles. Her stomach flipped. Swallowing hard, she
slowly drove up the U-shaped driveway and parallel
parked behind a cruiser and shut off her engine. Any
hopes that Evan had given her the wrong address dissi-
pated. She stepped from her car and moved to the back
of her vehicle. Everything she needed was in the trunk.
She pressed the button on her fob to unlock the trunk
so she could gather her supplies, her hands trembling
so hard she dropped her keys twice.

Cops with somber faces streamed out of the house.
They'd lost one of their own. Tracy had been with the
department a little under two years. Behind them, two
paramedics wheeled a stretcher. There was a body bag
on it.

Lissa slumped against the side of her car, tears dripping off her face. Tracy. What had happened?

One of the cops, Lieutenant Kathy Bartlett, caught
her gaze and headed in her direction. The sergeant had
been Tracy's mentor, she remembered. Emotionally raw,
Lissa fought the urge to hide and stood her ground.

"Lissa." Lieutenant Bartlett halted in front of her, her
features stiff, only her eyes displaying the deep grief
whirling inside her.

"It's Tracy. I know."

The sergeant nodded. "Yes. I'm sorry. Maybe someone else should do this."

Even though Lissa wasn't part of the police department, she'd met most of Tracy's coworkers. They all

knew she and Tracy were practically sisters, their bond was so close.

Lissa shook her head. It was the last service she'd ever do for her best friend. "There is no one else. I'll deal. How…"

Her mind couldn't process the question.

"I can't give you the details yet. We haven't even notified her family. When I can, you'll know."

It was the best she'd get.

While the cops and investigators closed down and began to depart the scene, Lissa gathered the supplies she'd need. Her limbs were like lead as she put on her protective gear and pulled her hair back into a ponytail. She struggled to get the latex gloves over her shivering hands.

A second vehicle pulled up behind her. She turned and saw Gage Wilson, the other cleaner. They nodded at each other. He hopped out and grabbed the biohazard disposal containers from the back of his truck. Lissa followed him into the all-too familiar house, with the cleaning agents in hand. For once, Gage didn't make any jokes. His unusual sensitivity pierced her already shaky armor.

Her insides quaked as they entered through the front door. The foyer area was immaculate. She could picture Tracy running out to greet her.

It would never happen again. Lissa tightened her jaw and gave her head a single hard shake, forcing herself to focus on the job at hand. An invisible fist squeezed her lungs. She had to get through this. *Please, God. Help me.*

Turning the corner into the kitchen, she froze. It was

always horrible seeing blood at a crime scene. This was so much worse. She'd never forget the sight of her best friend's blood on the kitchen floor.

"I don't think we need to make any zones today," Gage commented.

She blinked at him. "What?"

He frowned. "Well, this is the only part of the house affected, right? It's not too bad. No need to separate it. Say, are you hearing me all right?"

She blew out a breath. "Sorry. A little distracted."

She wouldn't tell him the truth. There was something about Gage she'd never trusted. The less conversation they had, the better. She blocked everything from her mind and brought out the cleaners to remove all the blood and stains from the floor and the spatter from the edge of the cupboards. There were no rugs, so the process was smooth. Every second burned in her mind, though.

"I'll take these out." Gage hefted the biohazard containers. "Did you bring in the ATP?"

She nodded and pointed to the portable device. It used fluorescent lighting to seek out any blood spatter on the surfaces. "I'll run it quickly."

She scanned the entire room. Her gaze rested on the narrow door on the far side of the kitchen. She grimaced. "We've got it all in here. We should check the pantry."

Please let him volunteer. Lissa had a violent fear of small places, dating back to an event in third grade when two bigger girls locked her in a tiny storage room at school, and Tracy's pantry was smaller than a walk-in closet. She was not going in there, but neither did she care to remind Gage of her phobia. He'd do it, but he'd remind her that he did it every chance he got. He was just that way.

"Oh, I'll get it."

Relieved, she waited until he returned and gave her a thumbs-up. "We're all done, then."

She scanned the entire room. "We've got it all."

"Okay. I'll see you back at the office."

She nodded and started packing up the rest of the supplies. Finishing, she sealed up the bin. The back of her neck prickled. Spinning, her eyes swept over the familiar room. Except for her, the room was empty.

Still, she felt invisible eyes watching her.

Twitching her shoulders, she turned back to her work. No one was here. Gage had left. As soon as she completed the job, she'd be out, too. Then she'd let herself grieve.

Her watch buzzed. She glanced down and grimaced. She had forgotten to text the babysitter that she'd be late picking up Shelby.

She sent her a text, guilt bruising her conscience. How had she forgotten Shelby? Sliding her phone back into her pocket, she bent back over the bin. The afternoon sun glinted off something in the corner of the room, under the edge of the sterling silver refrigerator. Moving closer, she gasped as recognition dawned.

A shadow alerted her to danger. She dodged the blow. Instead of hitting her head with killing force, the lead crystal vase glanced off her shoulder. Alyssa screamed in fear and pain. She looked into the eyes of a killer and let out another shriek a scant second before the next blow knocked her out.

* * *

Deputy US Marshal Micah Bender drove up the nearly empty driveway and parked close to the front lawn. Aside from the crime tape gently waving, the house was the epitome of a peaceful Ohio suburban residence. Checking his weapon one last time, he exited his SUV and locked it. As he approached the front end, he inspected the front tire. Was it low? He leaned closer, then froze as a shriek sounded inside the house. He abandoned his SUV and tore across the front lawn. A second scream split the air, abruptly cut short. Leaning forward, Micah pumped his arms to force his body to move faster and pounded toward the house. Yellow crime scene tape blocked his path. Without pausing to consider whether he should or not, he leaped over it. The local law enforcement and the crime scene investigation team had departed nearly two hours earlier. The only people here would be the crime scene cleaners.

But he only saw one car. And he knew who drove it.

Alyssa Page was the only authorized person on the premises. He'd talked with her merely a handful of times, but those screams couldn't belong to anyone else.

Bursting through the front door, he charged down the hall and into the kitchen. Alyssa was lying on her back, her thick dark hair matted and blood dripping onto the floor from a wound on her temple. The bin with her equipment was on its side next to her. A foot away from her, Micah saw the instrument used to bring her down. A lead crystal vase, the side splattered with her blood. The sight knocked the breath out of him. Alyssa Page was a sassy spitfire, always in motion. To see her unconscious and helpless shook him down to his foundation.

Assessing the scene, he looked for any immediate dangers. Not seeing any, he released the catch on his gun harness to give him instant access to his weapon and dropped down beside her, making sure his back was to the wall and his face was towards the kitchen entrance. He would be no use to her if he was caught unawares. Reaching out, he found the pulse on her neck. Good and strong.

Relief washed through him. He brushed her dark hair away from her temple. Blood continued to well and seep from the wound, but the flow had slowed, and it didn't appear deep. He left her side long enough to cross the room to the drawers on either side of the double sink. He opened them until he found the dish towels. Grabbing a clean cloth, he returned to her side and knelt. He gently pressed the white dish towel against the injury. A deep crimson blot appeared and spread over the pristine surface. Alyssa flinched and groaned.

He mentally sent a prayer of thanksgiving. She wasn't awake, but neither was she completely unresponsive. Bending over, he placed an arm next to her and braced himself, getting low and visually scanning what was visible of her head and neck. When he found no other wounds, he sat back on his heels. Then he remembered she had two cochlear implants. Most people wouldn't know they were there, but he happened to see the one the first time they talked when she brushed her hair back. She saw him looking at it and explained what the small black circles on either side of her head were. It had never occurred to him that he'd one day need to know that information. Moving his fingers gently along the sides of her head, he searched for both of her processors. They were still in place. That was good. He wasn't sure what kind of complications could arise if the attacker had hit on either surgery site.

He frowned. Head injuries were always risky. She'd need scans to make sure there wasn't serious damage. He grabbed his phone to dial 911. A sound halted him.

The killer was still in the house.

Micah grabbed his gun and shifted his stance so he was crouching over Alyssa. He couldn't take the chance of leaving her unguarded. What if the killer had an accomplice? Keeping his voice, he called in his location.

"Send backup and an ambulance," he whisper yelled into the phone.

"Ambulance will be there in ten, Deputy Marshal. Local backup is on the way."

He barely noticed the formal title. Most of the time, he and the other deputy marshals were just called marshal, unless their boss was in the room. Then that title belonged to him.

The front screen door banged shut. The perp was getting away.

He waited a minute, when nothing else happened, Micah dashed to the window. He caught the shadow of a motorcycle careening around the corner and down the street away from the house.

"The perp's on a black motorcycle. I can't see the make or the license plate from this angle." Micah spat out the name of the alley and the direction, but he knew it would be too late. Even if he ran to his SUV and gave chase, he doubted he'd catch the man.

And he wouldn't leave Alyssa alone, not when she couldn't defend herself.

Casting one last look down the alley, he left his post at the window and returned to her side. He removed his jacket and covered her body with it to keep her warm.

"Hold on, Alyssa," he told her. "Help is on the way. I'll stay with you until it gets here."

She was so small and fragile looking. When she was standing next to him, the top of her head came to his chin. He knew better than to underestimate her, though. She'd worked a very messy crime scene he'd been at a year ago. The level of focus and efficiency she'd displayed had stood out a mile, especially next to the young man working with her.

Since then, he'd been in her presence three times. Had he been in the market for a girlfriend, he might have even asked her out.

He wasn't, though. His entire life focused on his job. Eighteen months ago, the woman he loved had been stalked and murdered. Micah couldn't let it go. Not only had Penny been his fiancée, but she had also been his colleague. Six months ago, a second woman, this time an assistant district attorney, had been murdered on her birthday near Cleveland. He knew the man responsible for both women's deaths was still out there, somewhere. The case had grown cold.

Until today.

Officer Tracy Huber had been murdered in her kitchen, a week after her birthday, and a birthday card had been left next to her body. The assistant DA had been murdered in her office. A homemade birthday card had been left beside her head.

Exactly like the one that had been placed next to Penny's body.

Somehow, Alyssa had gotten involved. Had she seen the killer?

Voices interrupted his thoughts. The backup had arrived. Micah left Alyssa in the capable hands of the paramedics and joined the local law enforcement in sweeping the grounds, hunting for clues.

He wasn't deterred when they came up empty-handed. He was on the hunt. Sooner or later, the perp would get lazy or overconfident and make a mistake, and he'd catch him when he did. First, he needed to interview Alyssa. If she saw the perp, then the man could be behind bars before nightfall.

The front door opened. Alyssa was wheeled out on a stretcher. Her eyes were open. The moment the sun hit her face, she winced and scrunched them closed. Could be a concussion, with a reaction like that.

He jogged to her side. "Alyssa?"

She blinked up at him. "Marshal Bender?" A funny expression crossed her face. "What happened? Why am I on a stretcher? And why are you here?"

The bottom dropped out of his stomach. She didn't remember anything that had happened. Which meant Penny and Tracy's killer was still at large. If Alyssa had seen him, she now had a target on her back.

It was up to him to keep her safe until her memory returned.

TWO

The left side of her head pounded and throbbed like someone was using it for a bass drum. Voices and electronic chirps and beeps mingled around her. She couldn't make sense out of it. Lissa dragged her eyelids open and squinted against the harsh halogen light glaring down on her. Where was she? She twisted her head to the left and pain zigzagged through her skull. Clenching her jaw, she held still until the agony receded enough that she could catch her breath.

Slowly to avoid triggering any more sharp, stabbing pains, she moved her head to the side. One inch, then two, until she finally caught sight of her environment. She recognized the curtained-off cubicle and the medical devices surrounding her and the narrow, uncomfortable bed. She was in Sutter Springs Memorial Hospital. In the emergency room, to be exact. She sucked in a breath, shocked. How had she ended up here? She jerked upright, forgetting her injured head, then cried out and halted, sinking back into the limp excuse for a pillow, her head throbbing. Especially her left temple. And her shoulder. Obviously, she'd been in an accident of some kind.

Her heart pounded in her chest. Where was Shelby? Had her little girl been in the accident with her? Unable to remember the details, Lissa panicked. Gritting her teeth against the pain, she lurched to a sitting position and swung her legs over the side of the bed. She sat, gasping, and waited for the room to cease rotating around her. She couldn't remember ever feeling so weak or disoriented.

At least she was dressed in her own clothes and not a hospital gown.

The curtain whooshed open and the emergency room doctor entered, followed closely by a nurse. She didn't wait for them to speak. Her words tumbled over each other. "What happened? Is Shelby okay? Where's my daughter?"

The doctor held out his hands, motioning for her to calm down. "Slow down, Miss Page. You were brought in on an ambulance an hour ago. As far as I know, your daughter's fine. According to the police report, you were working. She wasn't with you. What do you remember?"

Her legs bounced as she gripped the side of the bed. Hadn't she already indicated she remembered nothing? Her muscles relaxed. Shelby wasn't hurt. That was the important thing.

"I don't know what happened." This was ridiculous. Clamping her hands on the frame on either side of her hips to steady herself, she slid off the mattress. The room tilted. She hung on and leaned back, praying her knees wouldn't buckle.

"Whoa! Hold on, there." Her eyes shot open as warm hands steadied her. She knew that voice. Opening her lids, she glanced up into the eyes of Deputy Marshal Bender. She'd only spoken to him a few times, but she recognized his voice. Micah Bender was only one of the many deputy marshals appointed to the southern Ohio district. He was the only one she knew by name, though.

He helped her ease back onto the bed, then remained until she was steady enough to sit on her own. She was too surprised to argue. What was bad enough that a deputy US marshal felt he needed to check on her personally?

"What's the last thing you remember?" He moved back, giving her some space.

The doctor scowled at Deputy Marshal Bender, but the other man ignored him. His piercing blue eyes remained trained on her. It was unsettling.

She turned her thoughts back to his question. "Is this still Wednesday?"

"Yes."

Well, she hadn't forgotten too much. "Okay." Closing her eyes, she cast her mind back over her day. "I dropped Shelby off at the babysitter at ten. I had the day off and a few errands to run. I'd planned to meet my best friend Tracy for her birthday lunch —"

A memory hit her with the force of a truck slamming into her and her voice died in her throat. "Tracy."

She couldn't breathe. Tracy was dead. She'd been called in to the crime scene. She opened her mouth wide, her lungs desperate for air, but her muscles refused to obey.

An arm around her shoulder brought her back. Deputy Marshal Bender was there, holding her upright. "Breathe, Alyssa. Breathe."

"No one calls me Alyssa."

The inane comment popped out without thought. He didn't need to know that. It was irrelevant. Tracy was gone.

"I was going to meet my best friend Tracy for lunch. Tracy Huber. She's a cop. We always treat each other out to celebrate our birthdays. Her birthday was last week."

Micah Bender stiffened, his eyes narrowed on her face. "Please go on."

Lissa paused. When he didn't speak, she wiped away the moisture gathering on her lashed and continued. "She never showed up. I left the restaurant and got a call from my boss, Evan. The moment I heard the address, I knew."

She choked and had to stop.

The marshal eased away from her but remained by her side. She shivered without the warmth of his arm across her shoulders.

"I know this is painful, Alyssa. I'm sorry. It's important. What happened when you got to the crime scene?"

She shook her head, slowly, suddenly numb. "I don't know. I have no memory of the crime scene. I remember waking up briefly and seeing you staring down at me. But the time between Evan's phone call and that moment is blank."

"Do you know if you worked the scene alone?"

She furrowed her brow, recalling Evan's phone call. "You know, I remember Evan saying that Gage Wilson was on his way to the crime scene. Evan doesn't like any of us on a crime scene alone. I honestly can't tell you if I saw him there or not. I assume he showed up at some point, although Gage is not the most reliable. His work ethic is sometimes lacking."

Lissa ground her teeth and tried to recall if she'd seen her coworker or not. It was no use. All she got for her effort was a sore jaw. She'd always scoffed at books and movies that used the amnesia trope. After all, she'd never known a single real case of it. Now she did. The looming emptiness of that short block of time curdled her stomach.

"What does it mean?" She met his blue gaze, trying to find the answers.

"It means you have a head injury," the doctor interrupted. "I'm sorry, Marshal Bender, I know you have an investigation to conduct, but this woman needs a CT scan on her head and an X-ray on that shoulder."

Micah made a sound that came really close to a grunt. Her eyes widened. Maybe she'd heard him wrong. A quick glance at his stoic face convinced her she hadn't. He was a man of few words. One could almost think him cold. She didn't, though. She didn't know anything about his life beyond that he was stationed in the area. His eyes, though, were tormented. His was a soul in need of healing.

"I'll be right outside in the waiting area. No one will enter the emergency room without me knowing about it."

Wow. Intense.

Why? Her shoulders stiffened. He thought she knew something. Or rather, she suspected he believed she was still in danger. She wanted to question him, but held back, unwilling to discuss the situation in front of others. She'd wait.

But first…

"Marshal Bender, could you call my babysitter? Let her know what's happening?"

When he nodded, she gave him Ginger's number.

"I'll take care of it." He backed out of the cubicle. The curtain swooshed closed behind him. The space seemed bigger without him.

She wrenched her gaze from where Micah had left and refocused on the doctor. "Can I have a CT scan? I wear bilateral cochlear implants. Would it be safe?"

She'd heard that prior to an MRI, sometimes the magnetic component of the processor needed to be surgically removed. Of course, that was probably more for older models, but she didn't want to take any chances. She wasn't sure about CT scans.

He nodded. "Yes, you don't need to worry. It won't hurt them."

Relieved, she agreed to proceed.

It was going on dinnertime before the doctor agreed to release her. He wanted to keep her overnight, but Lissa wasn't having it. Although her scans showed she might have a slight concussion, she had a daughter at home who needed her, and her babysitter had a life that included a second job. While Ginger's job was online, making it convenient for her to watch Shelby at a moment's notice, she deserved uninterrupted time to complete projects or see friends and family. Lissa refused to take advantage of her friend's generosity any more than necessary.

"I'm still not comfortable with this," the doctor began for the third time. "You were hit over the head and have some memory loss. However, I can't force you to stay."

"Thank you. I understand what you're saying, but I have responsibilities."

She hopped off the bed and left the cubicle before he revoked his permission. She slapped a hand against the swinging door and moved into the lobby area. Micah Bender was waiting for her. The moment their eyes met, he pocketed his phone and strode in her direction.

The expression on his face told her he was done waiting.

Micah searched her exhausted face. She needed rest. Her left temple sported a large, deep purple bruise. Her arm seemed stiff, too, so he figured she had some tissue bruising on her shoulder. She wasn't wearing a sling, though, so apparently it wasn't that bad. Other than two injuries, she appeared physically fine.

What struck him the most was the grief pulling her mouth down and shadowing her eyes. It would take a long time to heal from the loss of her friend. Not that one ever completely healed. It was more a matter of moving on and remembering how to live again.

He still hadn't figured that part out.

The waiting room was beginning to fill up. They couldn't have a conversation here. "I'll give you a lift home. We can talk in the car."

She shook her head. "I left my car at the…at Tracy's house."

Her face paled. She'd almost referred to her friend's home as the crime scene. He didn't correct her.

"Can we get it tomorrow? You probably shouldn't be driving tonight."

"Maybe. But I still need to get Shelby's booster chair."

He'd forgotten about that. He gestured for her to precede him. "Fine. We'll swing by and get the seat on the way."

As she passed him, he glanced down at her bare ring finger. All of a sudden, it struck him how little he knew her. She tended to keep to herself, and he didn't exactly encourage people to open up to him. Was she divorced or widowed? Not that it mattered. He was too broken to consider a relationship with any woman, no matter how captivating she was. And a woman who'd nearly been murdered at her best friend's murder scene was definitely out of the question.

Leading her out to his SUV, Micah assisted Alyssa in the vehicle. It was a high step, and she seemed a touch wobbly. When he was sure she was inside, he closed the door and strode around to the driver's side. He slid behind the wheel and started the engine, mentally considering how to begin the conversation. He didn't want to cause her more pain, but he needed the information she possessed.

"Why were you at Tracy's?" she asked suddenly. "I didn't think US marshals got involved with local crimes."

"They don't. This isn't a local crime." He paused. He only had a theory, but he believed it was the correct one. "I think this is connected to other murders. I don't know for certain, but I think we may be dealing with a serial killer. One who targets women in law enforcement. He leaves a birthday card next to the body. My initial thought was he killed them on their birthday."

She gasped. "Deputy Marshal Bender—"

He shook his head. "Marshal Bender is fine. I'm never called Deputy Marshal. Micah would be better, since we're both professionals."

She blinked. "Micah, then. Tracy's birthday was last week, though."

Checking his mirrors, he backed out of his space, then began the short drive to Tracy's house. "I know. That's why I'm rethinking my theory. It could be he kills them near their birthday. I don't know his timeline. Within a week? Their birthday month? I'm still not sure."

"You said he left a birthday card?"

He nodded. "We can't exactly trace the cards. In both previous instances, it was a handmade card. But yes, that is why we believe it's the same killer." He hesitated. She'd find out about Penny soon. And about the second victim. He opened his mouth to tell her but changed his mind and snapped his jaw closed. She had enough to deal with at the moment. A lot to process. Knowing those facts wouldn't help her. In fact, if she knew what they were up against, he doubted she'd get any sleep tonight. And unless she remembered more about the crime scene, it was unlikely she'd be able to help.

No, she'd learn all the gruesome facts soon enough.

"Micah, I hope you're wrong. The thought of a serial killer in our small community is beyond terrifying." Her brow crinkled. "But why did he attack me? I'm not in law enforcement, nor is it my birthday."

Micah turned onto Tracy's street and drove past the construction equipment at the top of the hill. The city was planning on demolishing the abandoned building

on the corner and building more family homes. He'd
seen it on the local news the evening before. The crane
with the wrecking ball was already in place, ready to be
put to use in the morning. He pulled his SUV behind her
small sedan. "Well, you work with law enforcement on
crime scenes, so maybe that's close enough. Honestly, I
was hoping you'd be able to remember what happened.
I believe you might have seen something or witnessed
something that put you in danger."

She chewed her lower lip. He found the action distracting and withdrew his gaze, choosing to stare out
the window.

"I don't remember anything about the crime scene
or the killer," she finally admitted. "But I do wonder if
he'll come after me again."

He wondered the same thing. "I won't abandon you.
I plan to stick to you like glue until he's caught."

She blushed and ducked her head. When her fingers
brushed her dark hair back behind her ear, the round
black processor caught his gaze. He hadn't seen her
cochlear implants this close before. The round disc attached to the side of her head was linked by a short
wire to what looked like a behind-the-ear hearing aid
without the ear mold.

"If you give me your keys, I'll get the car seat for
you," he offered.

She threw him a smile. "No, it's fine. I can do it.
Thanks anyway."

Throwing open the car door, she jumped down and
moved in front of his car. He approved of how she
looked both ways before moving up beside her car. One
could never be too careful. He heard the electronic beep

of her car doors unlocking. Her trunk also popped open. She grabbed a pink camouflage backpack and tossed it to the side before moving to the car to gather the seat.

A swift glance in the mirrors and quick sweep of the landscape revealed no dangers. He pulled his phone out of the cupholder and swiped through his text messages. So far, there was no news on the perp. Disappointing, yes, but not surprising. However, Micah had hope that this time they'd catch him.

He'd be able to find justice for Penny at last.

Maybe then, the guilt he'd worn like a shield for so long would fade.

First, he'd failed his sister, Joss, when she was abducted all those years ago, and then his fiancée, Penny, had been murdered. He was grateful that his sister had been returned to his family. And although she was *Englisch* now, like him, most of his Amish family had renewed their relationship with Joss.

A distant boom caught his attention. Raising his head, Micah peered into the rearview mirror. His jaw dropped. The wrecking ball had dropped from the crane and was rolling down the hill.

Alyssa hadn't noticed. It was going to flatten her in a few seconds.

Jumping from his vehicle, he raced over to the woman. She turned her head and her eyes flared wide. He grabbed her around the waist and flung both of them and the car seat into the grass on the other side of his vehicle, then used his back to shield them.

The wrecking ball clipped his bumper and slammed into her car. Glass shattered and small shards rained down upon them. Alyssa buried her face deeper into his shoulder, shaking. His side absorbed the moisture from the grass, but he didn't move until the car had ceased creaking and groaning.

Finally, he shifted off Alyssa and sat up before helping her do the same. His bumper was dinged up, but that seemed to be the extent of the damage. Alyssa's car was nearly flattened on the driver's side. The metal had been pounded and remolded, creating a nest for the wrecking ball.

"If you hadn't pulled me out of the way, I'd be dead."

Micah shuddered, horrified by the image her words evoked.

"Let's get you out of here." He stood and pulled her to her feet. He picked up the car seat. She paused briefly to collect the bag she'd chucked out of the car. Once they were in his vehicle with the car seat, he placed a call to the local police chief, Chief Spencer. Spencer heard him out as he explained the events of the day.

"I'm going to go out on a limb and say it's highly unlikely this was an accident."

"I agree sir. I think whoever killed Tracy had something to do with it."

Alyssa shifted beside him. He wished he could protect her from this, but she had a right to know what was happening.

"Are you taking Lissa home?"

Lissa? He recalled her saying most people didn't call her Alyssa. However, she hadn't objected, and she looked like an Alyssa to him. "I am. I'm planning on keeping watch tonight."

"Good plan. Bring her around to the station in the morning. I want to talk with her personally."

He disconnected and drove toward the babysitter's house. He hadn't been kidding when he'd said he planned on staying close. Whether she liked it or not, he was her personal shadow until the man responsible was behind bars.

He wouldn't fail again.

THREE

A thick silence filled the vehicle on the way to the babysitter's house. Micah sent several concerned glances Alyssa's way during the drive. All the blood appeared to have drained from her face, leaving her skin pale. He frowned. Was she going into shock? When their gazes met, her pupils weren't dilated. Her deep honey brown eyes were grief-stricken, but other than that, they appeared normal.

The only words she spoke consisted of directions. For the first few minutes, he had tried asking questions, but all he'd received for his efforts were single-word responses. After four such attempts, he gave up. If she didn't want to talk, he could respect that. She'd had a horrible day. Another glance provoked another worry. She might have been in pain, or suffering effects from her head wound. Being thrown to the ground couldn't have helped, although there had been no other way to keep her from getting squashed by the wrecking ball.

His questions would wait for morning.

When he pulled into the babysitter's driveway, Alyssa freed herself from the seat belt before he'd shifted to Park and flew to the front door of the house. By the time he'd turned off the engine and joined her, a small girl of about five was tucked in her embrace. The child was a miniature of her mother, from the rich brown hair and honey-colored eyes to the dimple in her right cheek when she smiled.

Shelby Page was going to be a heartbreaker in a few years.

"Mama, Ginger let me have pizza and ice cream for dinner." The little girl bounced on her toes and held on to her mother's denim jacket, her face alight with joy.

Apparently, this was not a normal occurrence.

Alyssa chuckled. It was a forced laugh, but it fooled her daughter. "Pizza and ice cream? It sounds like you two girls had a party without me."

Her dark eyes swept up and met those of the woman standing behind Shelby. Ginger smiled and nodded. "She was no trouble. It was actually frozen yogurt."

"It works." Alyssa popped one last kiss on the top of her daughter's head. "Get your stuff, Sweet Pea. It's time to go home."

But Shelby had noticed him. She pressed herself against her mother, her eyes huge in her tiny face. "Who's that Mama? And where's your car?"

"This is my friend, Micah, Shelby. He gave me a ride because my car, um, had a little accident."

A little accident? Micah's eyebrows climbed his forehead. He kept his mouth shut. Today's events weren't easily explained to a five-year-old. Shelby ducked out of her mother's arms and raced into the house to do as her mother instructed.

"Now that she's gone, what really happened?" Ginger asked, her voice soft.

Alyssa's gaze never left her friend's face. It took Micah a moment to realize she was reading her lips. Alyssa rarely missed a beat. It was easy to forget she didn't always hear what was going on. He'd heard female voices tended to be more difficult because they were pitched higher.

"Tracy's dead."

Ginger's face paled. Tears pooled in her eyes. Without a word, she reached out and hugged Alyssa, who sagged in her arms for a moment. Her shoulders shook, but she didn't make a sound. After a minute, she pulled back and wiped her arm across her wet face. Micah had to admire how quickly she brought her emotions under control.

"Honey, what happened?"

Alyssa shook her head at Ginger's question and tossed him a pleading glance. He took in her clenched jaw and knew she was holding it together by a thread.

"She was murdered," he breathed on a whisper. "That's all we know."

Whatever Ginger might have said, she swallowed it when Shelby reappeared. With a final hug, Alyssa gathered her happily chatting daughter and helped her settle into his SUV. "You can just drop us off at my house."

He shook his head. "No, I can't."

"Micah."

"No." He narrowed his eyes at her. "I said I plan to stick to you like glue, and I meant it. You aren't safe. Not yet. My boss already knows I'm working this case.

I got a call this morning from your CSU because of the birthday card left on the scene."

She opened her mouth. He edged closer to forestall her argument. "Alyssa, if there's one thing I know about serial killers, they escalate. I don't know how quickly, but this killer has now killed three times in the past eighteen months. All three women worked with the legal system in some way." He paused. Sharing personal information wasn't his favorite thing to do, but he could see the anxiety and fear lurking in her eyes. She deserved to know everything. "The first victim was a deputy marshal. She was my partner. And my fiancée."

She gasped, her hand flying to her mouth.

He hurried on, needing to get past Penny. "She and the other victim prior to today were both murdered on their birthdays. I need to talk with Chief Spencer. Try and figure out our next move. If you saw something, you might be all that stands between the killer and his agenda. Whether you like it or not, you are at risk. Look, I'll try not to get in your way. I just need a couch. Then tomorrow morning, we'll head to the police station. The chief will hopefully have a better plan for keeping you safe until this killer is off the streets."

Her lips tightened. He watched the struggle play out on her pretty features. She wanted to refuse. Alyssa Page was an intensely private person. He was only beginning to realize how much so. Letting herself lean on someone else had to go against the grain. Her eyes shifted to the back seat. In the rearview mirror, Shelby was talking to her stuffed pony. That was when he knew he'd won the argument. No matter how much it galled her, Alyssa would do whatever she needed to in order to protect her little girl.

"I don't think I have a choice." She lifted her gaze to his. "Whoever is behind this might try to hurt my daughter. I can't take that chance."

"I'll protect her. And you. That's my first priority." He infused as much confidence into his voice as he could. In the back of his mind, though, a small voice of doubt whispered he hadn't been able to protect Penny.

Alyssa jerked her face away and stared out the window.

By the time they arrived at her house, his stomach was rumbling like a bulldozer. It had been hours since he'd eaten. He should have suggested they stop and pick something up on the way. He'd been so focused on getting her safely home, though.

She directed him to park in front of the garage.

He raised an eyebrow. "Wouldn't it be safer to park in the garage?"

She lifted one shoulder. "It might be. However, I'm renting, and my landlord keeps his stuff in the garage. So, we don't have that option."

He made a mental note to talk with the landlord. Tomorrow. After parking his vehicle, he hopped out and jogged around to open Alyssa's door. She was already out of the SUV by the time he reached her. Without commenting, he opened the back door. She lifted Shelby out.

"What about the bag you grabbed from your car?"

She pivoted and stared at his SUV, chewing her full bottom lip. He averted his gaze. She was a distraction, no doubt about it. "I think we should leave the bag in your car. I always have an overnight bag packed for Shelby and me. I never know when I'll need to drop her off at Ginger's for the night, and sometimes, it's too late for me to come home, so I stay over. It's got clothes and a spare charger for my cochlear implant processors."

He nodded. "Yeah, leave it there."

He didn't say it out loud, but his gut said he needed to be ready in case they needed to move out suddenly. Maybe it was his years of training, but he went with his instinct. Better to be overprepared than unprepared.

He followed them to the house. Once she had the front door open, he took charge and searched the house quickly. It was a mark of how scared she was that she made no protests.

"I don't see anything suspicious," he informed her when he finished.

"Good. All the doors are locked. Let me get Shelby situated, then I'll get us something to eat. I'm starved."

He wasn't going to argue. Fifteen minutes later, they were sitting at the kitchen table eating grilled cheese sandwiches. It was the best food he'd ever eaten. By silent agreement, they didn't talk about what had happened. Shelby was too close.

Micah swallowed his last bite and rose to place his plate in the dishwasher. His phone rang. He glanced at the number and saw Chief Spencer's name. His boss, the top US marshal in their federal district, had arranged for him to work with the Sutter Springs Police Department. Showing the phone to Alyssa, he accepted the call.

"Hi, Chief. What's the news?" He winced. It probably wasn't professional to answer so flippantly, but he was exhausted, which meant his filter was a bit shaky.

"Micah. I had a couple of officers check on the wrecking ball. It had definitely been tampered with, as we expected. Lissa's car is totaled."

The feisty brunette wasn't going to be happy with that. On the positive side, she and her daughter were both alive. He was going to do everything in his power to make sure they stayed that way. There was no room for mistakes.

"We'll be by the station tomorrow morning."

"That's a plan. I'm assuming you're staying with her."

It wasn't a question. "Yes, sir. She's not leaving my sight until the killer is behind bars."

No matter how long it took.

Lissa tucked Shelby into her bed and kissed her, lingering a moment to inhale her daughter's fresh scent. A sob lodged in her throat. She choked it back. When she leaned away from her little girl, she kept a smile plastered on her face. The last thing she wanted to do was scare the child.

"Kiss Sonny, too, Mama." Shelby held her stuffed pony up. Lissa obliged her, then settled the toy back into her daughter's embrace.

"All right. It's time for all little girls and their ponies to go to sleep."

She rose from the side of the bed and left the room, keeping the door ajar so her daughter could see the hallway light. Making her way out to the living room, she halted in the doorway.

"Is everything all right?" Micah had a sheet spread out on the couch. He stood next to it, holding a pillow and blanket in his arms. He looked wiped out. Guilt swamped her. He had saved her life twice in less than twenty-four hours.

She nodded. "Everything's fine. I've triple-checked all the door and window locks. She's in bed. I'm glad you're staying tonight. Once I take my processors off and stick them in the charger, I'll be full deaf."

She'd also made sure all the blinds were closed and had placed a chair under the door handle leading to the garage. She crossed her arms. She didn't like letting people see her vulnerability. He needed to understand, though. Normally, she didn't worry about it. Tonight, she felt like there was a target strapped to her back. If only she could remember what she saw at the crime scene. Her eyes stung. She blinked. She'd shown enough weakness in front of this man. Hank had taught her men would take advantage of you and leave when you needed them most. Because of him, she'd left college and her dream of becoming a sous-chef and one day opening her own restaurant had disintegrated. She didn't have the money, or the support, to continue. That was before she was a Christian, and she knew there were good men out there. However, between Hank and Teddy, she didn't have the best record for identifying the good ones.

Micah crossed to her side and set his hands on her shoulders. "I'll be your ears tonight. Get some sleep." She searched his face. Lissa didn't trust easy, but this was one situation she couldn't handle on her own.

The tears she'd been fighting rose to the surface again. She was seconds away from disgracing herself with an emotional outburst that would mortify them both.

"Thanks." She cleared her throat and attempted to

smile. His eyes softened. Oh no. Sympathy was not what she needed at the moment.

Tugging away, she backed up. "I'm fine. See you in the morning."

His eyes narrowed, but he didn't protest. She turned and went to her room, closing the door gently behind her. Taking a deep breath, she grabbed her Bible and pulled it open, reading Psalm 23 to herself. It was the one she went to whenever she needed to remember that God was in charge and would never abandon her. When she finished, she replaced the Bible on the end table and got ready to sleep. Climbing into the bed, she reached up and removed the processors. Instantly, all sound ceased. Twisting the rechargeable batteries off, she attached them to the charger. She hesitated a moment before forcing herself to reach out and turn the light off. The room plunged into darkness.

She lay down and pulled the quilt over herself. Finally, she broke and shoved her face into the pillow. Unable to hold the pain back any longer, she let the pillow absorb the tears. She cried for Tracy, and she cried out her fear for Shelby and herself. Exhausted, she drifted off to sleep.

Someone was shaking her shoulders. Gasping, Lissa shoved the person away and bolted upright.

The light streaming through the door behind her revealed Micah. His lips were moving. All she saw were the words, "Leave now."

She felt a little dizzy. Shaking it off, she grabbed her processors and put them on. "What…"

His finger touched her lips. She stilled. "Grab Shelby. The carbon monoxide tester is going off."

She couldn't hear it.

Urgency flooded her system. Carbon monoxide. That was why she was feeling so dizzy. Running to Shelby's room, she threw open the window. Light was just beginning to edge its way over the horizon. She turned back to the bed and grabbed the little girl. Shelby woke, crying. "Come on, baby. We have to go. The alarm's going off."

They'd practiced leaving the house if an alarm went off. She had never thought they'd actually need to use the skills. Silent tears tracked down Shelby's cheeks, but the child didn't argue. Hooking her arms around her pony, Shelby reached for her mother. Lissa lifted the child in her arms and joined Micah in the hall. A slight headache was building behind her eyes. Another sign of carbon monoxide poisoning.

She smothered the fear and pressed Shelby's face into her shoulder, praying her daughter would be safe.

Micah pulled the front door open.

Her jaw dropped open. Through the early dawn, she saw the beam wedged against the screen door. This was no accident. Someone had trapped them in the house and filtered poisonous gas into the house.

If they could not get past the blocked door, it would be the last sunrise any of them would ever see.

Micah whirled away from the door and staggered into the kitchen. He returned with a chair. Motioning for her to step back, he smashed the chair through the picture window and swept the glass away from the bottom of the pane with the leg of the chair. Fresh air and cool rain brushed her face.

"We have to get out of here." Micah dropped the chair and carefully stepped out the window. Turning back, he motioned for her to hand him Shelby. The terrified child buried her face in her mother's neck and clung to her. Lissa pulled her daughter's arms away from her neck. Every moment they stayed, she and Shelby were in mortal peril. They needed to get out of the house.

Her daughter resisted for a moment until she said, "Honey, you have to. Mama can't get to safety until you do."

That worked. Her daughter let go and she handed the child into the deputy marshal's waiting arms. Micah settled Shelby in the crook of one arm and held out his other hand. Lissa grabbed it, feeling the strength of his grip. The moment her feet touched the earth, the adrenaline in her blood dipped and her knees buckled. He grabbed her and gathered her and Shelby close.

Just for a moment. The rain pelted them, soaking through their hair and nightclothes. They hadn't even had time to grab clothes.

"We have to go. We're sitting ducks out here."

She understood. The killer could be watching. Her neck prickled. She was certain his eyes were trained on them even now.

FOUR

They needed to move. Already, the sun was beginning to climb higher above the horizon and into the
cover of clouds. He glanced at his watch. It was 6:30
a.m. The falling rain was the only sound to disturb the
overcast morning.

Micah shoved his jacket back and checked his service weapon and the holster. He then released his jacket,
and it fell back into place. He'd be more comfortable
if he could hold the weapon, but the safety of the child
and woman at his side came first. Too many civilians
were injured every year because of moving around with
a loaded gun. His own brother, Isaiah, had been out
hunting with a friend when he was sixteen. The friend
had fallen on his gun and died in Isaiah's arms. Micah
winced at the memory. Isaiah had come home covered
with blood and unwilling to speak for over a week. The
only sound they heard from him during that time were
bloodcurdling screams that wakened the entire family
night after night. The nightmares eventually dwindled
in number, but his brother was never the same after that.
And who could blame him?

Less than a year later, Isaiah had walked away from Sutter Springs and the Amish community they'd lived in all their lives. Including their family. No one had seen or heard from him in the past eleven years.

Shaking himself free from the web of memories, he briefly touched Lissa's elbow. She nodded. Staying close to the shadows provided by the overhanging edge of the roof, he led them around to the driveway. Lissa took another step, advancing toward his vehicle. He held out an arm, blocking her way.

"Wait. I want to make sure it's safe."

After a wrecking ball had landed on her car, he didn't want to take any chances. This perp was canny. He'd killed three women in less than two years, and they still didn't have any suspects.

"Mama…" Shelby's voice trembled between them. "I'm scared. I don't want to go in the car."

Lissa lifted her daughter in her arms and tucked Shelby's head under her chin. "I know, Sweet Pea. I am, too. But we'll be okay. God sent Marshal Micah to keep us safe."

Micah blinked. Part of him was touched. On another level, though, he was uneasy. There were some things you couldn't promise. Escaping a cunning killer was one of them. He'd do his best. Hopefully, it would be enough.

A lonely tear wound its way down the child's pale cheek. Despite his intention to remain aloof, he found her sadness slipping beneath his armor and wounding his heart. "Shelby, your mama and I are here. We won't leave you. But we have to move. Can you be brave for me?"

She thrust her bottom lip out in a pout and held a

well-loved brown stuffed pony close, resting her chin on the toy. He hadn't noticed the animal when he'd hefted her through the window.

When she nodded her head, he smiled at her.

Turning to his vehicle, he did a thorough search, checking underneath and in the wheel wells. "I don't see anything. Let's go."

He opened the back passenger door. Lissa rushed to the vehicle and put the wiggling Shelby in her car seat faster than he'd believed it was possible to. The belt clicked into place. Lissa backed out of the car and stepped out of the way to close the door, bumping into him in the process. Her warm breath hit the side of his face.

A shiver ran down his spine.

She was too close. Refusing to acknowledge the attraction simmering between them, he backed up and opened her door for her, using his body as a shield against any unseen assailants. She folded herself into the seat and leaned away from the door so he could close it.

The second the door was shut, he ran around to the other side and hopped inside. He pushed down on the brake and jammed the pad of his thumb against the start button. The engine roared to life. Micah shifted into Reverse and backed out.

Once they were on the street, he flipped the heat on high. Within two minutes, warm air poured from the vents and circulated through the SUV. "I have blankets, too, if you need them."

Lissa twisted her torso and peeked into the back seat.

"You all right, kiddo? Need one of Marshal Micah's blankets?"

It made him smile this time when she said his name. The way she phrased it, *Marshal Micah*, reminded him of his own family.

"I'm okay, Mama."

Lissa flopped back against her seat, sighing. She glanced over at him. "What has you smiling?"

He wiped a hand over his mouth, smoothing away the smile. "Sorry. I don't want you to think I take any of this lightly. I don't."

She shifted in her seat, angling her head and bringing her full attention to his face. "I would never think that. Especially not after the past seventeen hours or so. I don't really know what time it was that you found me." She waved a dismissive hand. "Doesn't matter. I've seen how seriously you take the safety of Shelby and myself. But if there's something amusing that you can share, I'd love to hear it. I could use something to take my mind off things."

He adjusted his hands on the steering wheel and checked the mirrors again. He wasn't one for talking and driving at the same time. But thanks to his sister's influence in his life, he was getting more comfortable with multitasking.

"It's nothing that private. You just sounded like my parents for a moment." He shot a glance her way to gauge her reaction. She didn't disappoint. Her forehead scrunched, and her lips were pursed. He grinned and relented. "I was raised in an Amish community. My district was outside of Sutter Springs, but we still had a Sutter Springs address."

"That's interesting. I still don't understand the connection."

"I'm getting there." His tires hit a puddle and a wave of water hit the already streaming windshield. Micah increased the intensity of the wipers for a moment to clear the excess moisture, then returned the wipers to medium. "In the Amish world, we don't refer to Mr. Bender or Mrs. Bender. Not among ourselves. The idea being no one should stand out. Hence, my dad is always Nathan. If there was another Nathan in the community, he'd be Carpenter Nathan. My *mamm* is Nathan's Edith, because there's another Edith around her age. My cousin Ruth is Teacher Ruth. She'll be married soon, though. Her fiancé lives in another district, so maybe she'll be just Ruth again." He shrugged. "It's not really that funny. There is another Micah in my district. If I were still there, we'd have been distinguished somehow. But I doubt 'Marshal Micah' would ever be heard in any Amish community."

She chuckled softly. "Probably not."

She bit her lip again.

"You have a question, don't you?" He guessed.

"It's rude." She shook her head.

"Now I'm really curious." When she remained silent, he took a hand off the wheel and nudged her arm. "Come on. I won't get mad. Promise. If I don't want to answer, I'll just tell you."

She turned her head to peek at Shelby. He flicked his gaze to the rearview mirror. The poor kid was zonked out. It had been a rough night. He'd do all he could to make her safe so she could go back to enjoying being a five-year-old.

"Okay. Well, I had always thought that if you left an

Amish community, you forfeited all contact with your family. But you obviously still talk with them. At least your cousin."

"You're right. It's rude."

A deep red tide swept over her smooth skin. Ducking her head, she whispered, "Told you. Sorry."

Instantly contrite, he touched her shoulder. She looked up at him. "I'm sorry. I was joking. Truly." He smiled briefly to show he wasn't offended. "In answer to your question, it's all a matter of timing. I left when I was almost eighteen. It was either that or become baptized. So, I was never an adult in the Amish church. My parents weren't happy with me, and for a time, our relationship was strained. But when my sister returned two years ago, we put our differences behind us."

"Your sister—"

He held up a hand. "Maybe I'll tell you someday, but that's not a story I want little ears to wake up and hear."

She nodded.

"So, you still see your family frequently?"

Was that wistfulness in her tone?

"I see them enough," he said. "My parents have the entire family out to their place the last Saturday of every month. It's getting crowded. My brother Zeke married, oh, about six months ago. He and his wife, Iris, own a house about ten minutes away from my parents' house. Joss, my sister, is married now. She and her husband, Steve, have a two-month-old baby."

"That's sweet. Are they your only siblings?"

He didn't know why he was answering all these questions. He never talked about his family while he was on the job. It tended to be a sensitive subject. He wasn't ready to let anyone outside his circle know about Joss's kidnapping years ago, or the drama with Isaiah. After the way his joke had backfired, though, he didn't want to embarrass her again.

"I have three brothers. Joss is my only sister."

He should have said two brothers. If she asked about them...

"Are they older or younger?"

His shoulders heaved with a sigh. There it was. "Younger. Zeke is twenty-nine, Isaiah—" just saying his name hurt "Isaiah is twenty-eight and Gideon and Joss are both twenty-six. Twins."

He waited for the next question. When it didn't come, he flicked a quick glance her way. She leaned forward slightly and frowned.

"What's that?" She pointed a trembling finger to the left corner of the windshield.

Micah followed the trajectory of her finger. A large black-and-white ATV with red decals and a bright red protective grill on the front burst out from behind the line of trees, driving in a parallel course with his SUV. Somehow, he didn't think it was accidental. Testing his theory, Micah pressed the gas down. The engine revved as more gas pumped through the vehicle and the speedometer rose from fifty-seven to sixty-one. The speed limit on the two-lane state highway was fifty-five miles per hour. He didn't want to go any faster on the wet road. With all the rain and the puddles, they'd run the risk of hydroplaning.

He sped up a couple more notches. The ATV followed suit.

No doubt about it. They were being followed.

* * *

Lissa clenched her hands together as the ATV continued to match speed with Micah's SUV. Rain pelted the windshield. Even on high, the wipers weren't able to keep up with the torrent hitting the vehicle and sloshing into puddles along the edges of the road and in the dips and potholes.

"I don't like this." Micah muttered.

Lissa leaned over and looked at the speedometer. "Micah! You're going over sixty miles an hour. How is he going that fast? ATVs can't move that fast."

Not to mention, how was this safe? The SUV hit a puddle and the vehicle shuddered. She saw Micah's grip tighten on the wheel, steering it to the left to remain on the road. Her stomach quivered.

"That's not your average off-road vehicle. Some of them can go much faster."

Micah reached out a hand and tapped the phone button on his dashboard to dial 911. His voice flowed too fast for her to catch all the words. She did get enough to know he'd called for backup. Which meant this was serious and not just some teenager being foolish. Her glance shivered between the grim man seated beside her and the ATV shadowing them.

Without warning, the ATV driver looked their way briefly. Lissa shivered, although she couldn't see his face beneath the black helmet with the dark visor. She cringed back against her seat until he removed his gaze from them and leaned forward. The ATV zipped up a slight hill and bounced over the flowing water in the drainage ditch. He passed them and flew ahead of Micah's SUV.

Lissa sighed, relaxing back into the seat. He hadn't been after her. He was probably some reckless teen who thought he was invincible and didn't realize how dangerous it was to drive that way in the rain.

Micah slowed down. His knuckles were white on the steering wheel. He was still tense, ready to react to a perceived threat. The muscles in her stomach knotted. She glanced back at her daughter. Shelby was awake, playing with Sonny quietly in her seat. Her innocent daughter had no concept that they could still be in danger.

Lissa returned her attention back to the ATV.

The daredevil driver swerved directly in their path, turning sideways and coming to a complete stop. Lissa braced her arms on the dashboard.

Micah stomped on the brake. The SUV skidded to a halt. The jolt sent her lurching toward the front of the car until the seat belt strapped across her torso tightened and stopped her forward motion. That was going to hurt later. When she raised her head, she felt as though all the air had been sucked from her lungs. The ATV hadn't moved. Its driver, however, had grabbed hold of a crossbow. Even while she watched, he grabbed the strangest-looking arrow she'd ever seen from a bucket of arrows sitting next to him and was rapidly fitting it into the bow. The tip, instead of the normal, pointed arrowhead, was shaped more like a honey pot with a razor shard point at the end.

"Hold on," Micah ordered.

"Mama, I'm scared!" Shelby screamed from the back seat.

"It's okay, Shelby! It'll be fine. Hold tight to Sonny."

Lord, protect my baby girl. Please. And Micah and me.
If it were safe, or if they had the time to stop, she'd
climb into the back to be with her daughter. But time
was something they didn't have.

Micah zoomed into Reverse, spinning the wheel
and careening the SUV to face the other direction. He
shifted into Drive and slammed his foot on the gas, ignoring the rain and the slick roads. Glancing into the
window on the side of the SUV, Lissa flinched as the
arrow was launched into the air. It stuck the ground beside the vehicle and exploded, sending chucks of earth
flying.

He was firing explosive arrows!

"Micah!"

"I know!"

A thin white line surrounded Micah's mouth. Shelby
was sobbing behind her. Her heart broke for her terrified
child, but there was nothing she could do until they'd
left this arrow-shooting maniac in the dust.

The ATV pursued them. She didn't know how he
managed to drive and continue to lob arrows in their
direction, but he did. Every thirty seconds or so, another one exploded. Most missed by a mile. A couple
came close, though. Too close.

How many arrows did he have?

Lissa twisted in her seat in time to see an arrow flying straight at them through the back window.

"Micah!"

The deputy marshal spun the wheel hand over hand
in an attempt to evade the incoming explosive. For a
moment, Lissa felt like the world moved in slow motion. She couldn't remove her gaze from the deadly pro-

jectile coming toward them with unerring accuracy. It dipped below the rear mirror. She could no longer see it. For an instant, she had hope.

She glanced in the side mirror as the rear passenger wheel erupted, flames shooting upward. Shelby! Lissa screamed. The vehicle spun in a wide arc, slipping on the wet pavement. Shreds of burning rubber remained on the street. The SUV was out of control. Lissa's stomach fell when the vehicle went airborne and left the road, sailing over the drainage ditch. It slammed to the ground on the other side, leaning at an awkward angle.

Their vehicle wasn't on fire, but neither were they out of danger. The ATV drove straight over the remains of the tire. The relentless driver notched another arrow, aimed the black crossbow and shot straight at them. The SUV rocked, and flames shot up, covering the back window. In her car seat, Shelby screamed.

"Move! We have to move now!" Micah shouted, releasing his buckle.

Lissa didn't argue. She leaped from her side of his SUV and attacked the back door, yanking it open and ripping her daughter from the wreckage. Shelby burrowed her head in her mother's hair, her tiny arms wrapped tightly around Sonny.

"Here."

Micah appeared at her side. She handed him her daughter. At the last minute, she grabbed the backpack holding their clothes and her spare charger before taking off after Micah. The ATV had stopped. Looking back over her shoulder, she stared into the dark visor. She knew he was staring at her. She only saw the visor. It creeped her out. His hand reached back. She had no doubt he was reaching for another arrow. They couldn't outrun it on foot. They'd have to dodge it.

Before his hand connected with the last arrow sticking out of the bucket, a siren shrieked, getting louder as it approached. Lights pierced the cloudy haze. She'd forgotten Micah had called for backup. The killer dropped the arrow and revved his engine, speeding in the opposite direction, zipping around a car coming toward them from the other direction. The small compact car slammed on its brakes and honked its horn. The ATV didn't even slow.

A black four-door police sedan sped past them, chasing after the killer on his ATV. A second police cruiser slowed and parked along the road, keeping its distance from the burning SUV. Micah grabbed Lissa's hand and pulled her further away. She'd stopped running once the police had arrived.

"Come on. That thing could blow if the flames hit the gas tank."

"That police car—"

"They know what they're doing. They've seen car fires before. Trust me, they'll be fine."

Trusting him wasn't as easy as he made it sound. It was a long time since she'd trusted any man. He held Shelby close and jogged over the wet, flat grassy terrain. She had no choice but to keep up with him.

They made it twenty feet before the SUV exploded behind them.

The blast sent heat washing over them and debris flying. Micah grabbed Lissa and pushed her down to the ground, using his own body to shield her and Shelby from harm.

FIVE

The sudden shriek of a fire truck and several emergency vehicles arriving on the scene shocked Lissa out of her stupor. Firefighters clambered off the engine, and a man with a white helmet left the cab of his truck to join them. He was the chief, she recognized, before returning her attention to the person who always came first with her. Ignoring the commotion around the burning vehicle near the road, she reached for her daughter. Shelby was silently weeping, giant tears dripping from her trembling chin. Lissa surveyed the child from head to foot. Aside from fear, Shelby appeared to be well. No cuts or scrapes were visible on her pale skin. As she clasped her daughter to her, she realized Micah still held them both in his embrace.

Lissa backed out of his arms. He dropped them without a word.

Glancing up into his eyes, Lissa forgot whatever comment she had planned to make. Rain dripped from his short, military-length sandy-blond hair. His taut jaw and tense mouth radiated pain. He had taken the brunt of the blast, she realized. While she and Shelby had felt nothing more than the jolt of hitting the ground and cold rain on their skin, Micah had left himself open to the heat and the chunks of metal hurled into the air. Around them, smoke rose from the wet grass in multiple places. Flames from the debris, put out by the pouring rain. Although she couldn't see any burns, that didn't mean he wasn't hurt in some way.

"Micah, are you all right? Are you hurt?"

Micah shook his head, perhaps more to clear it than in response to her concerns. He coughed twice into his elbow and grimaced. "Don't worry about me. I'm good. A piece of debris of some sort struck my back. Nothing I can't handle. The most important thing right now is that you and Shelby are unharmed."

She didn't necessarily agree with that assessment. Yes, she was glad that she and her daughter weren't hurt, but he had sacrificed his own safety to protect them. She wasn't sure how she felt about that. Guilt nudged its way into her soul. If he hadn't had to protect them, he would have been fine. She needed to try harder to remember the crime scene. If she could only recall it, maybe they'd know why she'd suddenly become a target.

"You can forget whatever it is that's going through your mind, Lissa." His stern voice cut through her the silence.

Startled, she lifted her face to his. "Nothing's going through my mind."

Her face burned at the obvious deception.

He scoffed. "Uh-huh. Yeah. Because you weren't just feeling bad that I got hurt. You have a very open face." He took a step closer. "Lissa, this is not your fault. Someone decided to chuck arrows at us. That's on them. I'm just thankful that we were able to keep ahead of him until backup came. Hopefully, the police will have caught the perp. I for one am looking forward to having a long conversation with him. Whoever puts a child in danger deserves to spend the rest of their lives in jail."

She nodded. They were on the same page there. "But Micah, you look like you're in pain."

He shrugged. "I'm doing my job and sometimes that means I get hurt." He glanced back over his shoulder. "Come on. My partner's here. Maybe he's got information."

She hadn't noticed the other deputy marshal arriving. Shelby wiggled. Reluctantly, she allowed the child to slide down her body and walk by her side. Her instinct was to shield her daughter from any danger and keep her as close as possible, but the truth was Shelby was getting too big to be carried around. Lissa sent up a silent prayer, asking God for His continued grace and guidance in their current situation.

Walking behind Micah, she frowned. The back of his jacket was a seamstress's nightmare. It was torn in several places, threads hanging loose, and two large holes where fabric wasn't merely ripped. It was completely missing.

They neared his partner. She hung back with Shelby as the two deputy marshals greeted each other. The first half of their greeting was so filled with law enforcement lingo, she couldn't have repeated it if her life depended on it. Finally, Micah half turned and waved her over.

Gripping her daughter's hand, she led her over to where Micah and his partner stood, keeping her gaze averted from what remained of his vehicle. Walking with Shelby pressed against her side presented a bit of a challenge, but she welcomed the comfort of her daughter's warmth.

"Lissa Page, this is Parker Gates, my partner."

She nodded a greeting to the other man.

Micah's partner had the brightest head of red hair she'd ever seen in her life. He was an inch or so shorter than Micah was, so she placed him between five foot eleven and six feet tall. He was dressed like Micah, in a dark suit and tie. But where Micah's handsome face was serious and shuttered, his partner greeted them with an easy smile creasing his lightly freckled face. She wasn't fooled by the neighborly welcome. His hazel eyes constantly roamed the terrain, intent on finding threats before they became a problem. She'd seen Tracy and Micah do the same.

Tracy. How could she forget her about Tracy? The events of the morning had chased all thought except escape and survival from her mind. Now that she and Shelby, and Micah, were safe, her soul was flooded with images of Tracy. The sorrow threatened to drown her.

"Hey." Micah stood in her path. "Hold tight for a few minutes more. We'll get a ride to the police station."

She swallowed to clear the tears clogging her throat away. "You need to be checked out by a doctor."

"Dude," his partner exclaimed, pointing at the back of his jacket. "She's not kidding. That has to hurt."

"I'm fine, Parker." Suddenly, Micah grinned. Lissa caught her breath. She'd never seen him smile like that before. "My car, on the other hand…"

Parker glanced over at the smoking remains and

whistled, shaking his head. "Yeah. Your ride is toast, buddy. You're not going to be able to fix that."

Peaking at the burning mess that had once been Micah's shiny and obviously pricey SUV, she shuddered. If he hadn't been helping her, he'd still have his car.

"We're not doing too well in the vehicle department, Micah."

He chuckled. "Yeah."

At Parker's questioning glance, he explained about Lissa's run-in with a wrecking ball. The laughter faded from his partner's face. "You're messing with someone really dangerous. And resourceful. You need to take care."

"We will."

'I'm here to help any way I can."

"Mama." Shelby tugged on her hand, whining. "Sonny's hungry."

Smiling, she leaned over and kissed Shelby's head. "Yeah? What do you think we should do about it?"

"I think he needs some waffles."

"With maple syrup?"

"Yes. Extra maple syrup. And chocolate milk."

Micah coughed again, barely disguising a chuckle. He winked at Lissa. "What do you think, Parker? Why don't you give us a lift to the precinct, then we can order some food?"

He probably thought he was being clever, weaseling his way out of having his back looked at. "That sounds perfect. After the paramedics clear you," Lissa said.

Micah narrowed his eyes at her. She scoffed at his intimidating glare and folded her arms across her chest. She was a single mother of an active five year-

old. She knew how to deal with defiance. "We'll wait."
She glanced down at her hungry daughter. "Sweet Pea,
Marshal Micah is hurt. Can we wait long enough for
someone to take of him?"

Shelby chewed on her thumbnail while she considered this new bit of information. "I am hungry," she finally declared. "But I don't want Marshal Micah to be
hurt. He can hold Sonny if it will make him get better."

The small child moved to stand in front of the tall
man who'd saved them and held her beloved toy out to
him. Micah's eyes widened, then his expression became
soft. He hunkered down in front of her, putting himself
at eye level, melting her heart a little more with his actions. Not everyone was patient with five-year-olds. She
had run into plenty of adults who let their disapproval
of her and the mistakes she'd made show in how they
interacted with Shelby. She was an intelligent child, but
she was sensitive as well.

"Thanks, sweetie. That means a lot to me. But I don't
need to take your pony. I think Sonny would rather stay
with you."

He stood up and ruffled her hair before heaving a
long-suffering, exaggerated sigh. He jerked his head
toward the EMTs starting to walk their way. "I better
get this over with."

He marched over to the EMTs. The crew had him
remove his jacket. His shirt under the jacket didn't look
torn up, which was good. She averted her gaze when
he lifted the back of the garment to give them a better
view. When she saw him a few minutes later, his shirt
was down again.

Below the short sleeve on his right arm, she saw what

looked like a number tattooed on the back of his arm. She'd seen such a tattoo before. It was a military tattoo. She couldn't tell which branch.

She didn't know why someone who'd grown up Amish would join the military. Whatever the reason, Micah was proving himself to be a rock. She was learning to trust him, in spite of her history.

Hopefully, she wouldn't regret it.

It was almost lunch time and they were still at the scene. They'd promised Shelby waffles, and he meant to make good on that promise. The kid had been a real trouper, not complaining after her initial whining that her "pony" was hungry. She drooped against her mother's side, worn out from lack of sleep and the waiting.

Micah stepped away from the professionals swarming the area and made a quick call to his boss, US Marshal Tim Hendrix, to inform him of the morning's events. When Hendrix asked what he needed, he told him he needed to move Lissa and Shelby to a safe place out of the open.

"Someone's targeting her, sir. I think she saw something at the crime scene."

"Which means the BCK was on-site."

Micah blinked. "Sir? BCK?"

A derogatory snort came through the phone. "Ridiculous, I know. It seems this guy is now being called the Birthday Card Killer."

"That's a disgusting name."

Micah felt sick. Birthday cards brought to mind fun and presents and joyful celebrations. Not death. But this killer had taken something innocent and turned it into something monstrous. He couldn't wait to put this killer behind bars.

"Yeah, it is. But that's what the press has dubbed him."

"How did the press get the information? I would have heard if Chief Spencer had mentioned it in a press conference."

"It wasn't the chief. Someone leaked the information to the press."

"Either the killer wants the attention or someone else has found the connection."

"Exactly. Micah, go to the Sutter Springs Police Department. You need to coordinate with them on this case. I know a multistate serial killer is more in our jurisdiction, but officer Tracy Huber was one of them. They need to be involved in every step."

"Yes, sir. What about Lissa Page and her daughter?"

"You'll need to coordinate a plan with the chief to keep her safe."

He could do that. If the department could keep her out of harm's way, it would provide him the opportunity to continue hunting. This killer, whom he refused to call him by the moniker BCK, had started to escalate.

He started to speak again when his brain caught up with his superior's cryptic words. His hand tightened around the phone under his fingers ached. Clenching his teeth around the words to keep his emotion in check, he spoke softly to Marshal Hendrix. Praying he'd misheard, already knowing he hadn't.

"Multistate? The murders have happened near Columbus and Cleveland."

"And Indianapolis. Two months ago."

"Why hadn't we connected that one earlier?"

"She was murdered outside. The birthday card must have blown away," Marshal Hendrix said.

Micah listened as the man filled him in on the details, appalled.

Four murders. Eighteen months ago, six months ago, two months ago, and yesterday. "He's escalating quickly."

"Yes, he is. The only consolation I can think of is that it's still April, for another two more days at least. The way he's speeding up his timetable, though, I think we should be alert for an attempt to find a May birthday victim."

Micah ran a hand through his hair, then swept it over the top to smooth it down again. Agitated, he began to pace. "We can't keep all women connected to law enforcement who have May birthdays holed up for the month of May. That's not practical."

"Agreed. And until we have an idea of where he'll go for his next target, we need to remain vigilant."

Hanging up, Micah searched for his partner. Pulling him off to the side, he related what their boss had told them.

"We need to get Lissa and Shelby to the police department now and begin pooling our data with theirs," Parker said.

Micah nodded. "We'll order something to eat, on our way. Shelby's been very patient."

His partner flashed him an amused glance.

"What?"

"You sound like a dad."

Micah scoffed. Chances of him ever becoming a father were slim to none. He didn't comment, though. Although Parker had his back and he trusted him like a brother, there were some parts of his life he didn't discuss.

Lissa stood the moment he and Parker approached her. He started to explain what they were doing, without going into all the gory details. She grabbed the pink camouflage backpack with one hand and held up the other one for Shelby.

"Will there be food?" She dipped her chin toward Shelby.

Micah nodded. "Yeah. We'll an order something on the way there. The chief will want to talk with you, go over what's been going on with the case."

Surprised, she tilted her head, considering his words. "Not that I'm complaining about having more information about what's going on. Because I'm not. Being kept in the dark is a little frustrating, although it's probably easier on my nerves not to know everything that's happening. But still, I'm realistic to know that you probably don't share case details with most civilians."

Nor did he want to get too specific out here in the open. "Little ears."

Lissa bit her lip, then nodded, shadows lurking in her eyes. Even if she didn't say it, he knew she was disturbed. Who wouldn't be? Her best friend had been murdered, her car had been crushed by a wrecking ball, they'd all been nearly poisoned while they were sleeping, and then they'd been run off the road by an ATV and explosive arrows. The past twenty-four hours had been more exciting than any action movie.

And the worst of it was, until they found whoever

was responsible, they'd have to keep looking over their shoulders.

Arriving at Parker's vehicle, Micah opened the back door and helped Lissa and Shelby climb into the back seat. Lissa strapped her daughter in with a tense smile.

"Mama, where's my booster seat?" Shelby chirped, cradling Sonny in her arms like a baby.

Lissa placed a soft kiss on her daughter's hair. "Sweet Pea, do you remember how we were driving with Marshal Micah? And his car caught on fire?"

Micah grimaced.

"Uh-huh. Someone tossed fire arrows at it." Shelby said, her little face serious. "Then BOOM!"

The child flung her arms wide to demonstrate the explosion, the pony dangling from her tiny fist.

The adults all shuddered. They'd come so close to being blown up with that car. It wasn't something they would ever talk about lightly. Lissa's expression became pained. He sympathized. As much as parents wanted to protect their children, life didn't always allow that to happen.

"Yes, Shelby. Your booster was in the car. It's no longer usable."

Shelby's bottom lip poked out. She gave an exaggerated wiggle under the seat belt. "It's not comfy anymore."

When Lissa's face grew distressed, Micah tapped her on the shoulder. He waited until she glanced at him. He mouthed, "She's alive."

Her head dropped. Momentarily, the top of her soft hair brushed his chin. When she raised her head again, the soft smile she aimed at him was more natural. "Thank you."

She was so close that if he bent his head, he could close the short gap between them and kiss her smiling lips.

What!? Since when did he think about kissing a woman he was protecting? The answer was never. He wasn't going to start now. He backed away and hopped in the front passenger seat before he did something he'd regret, such as giving in to the sudden impulse that had hijacked his brain for a second.

The driver's-side door opened. Whistling off-key, Parker entered the SUV and started the engine. Micah sighed, leaning back against the headrest. He'd never been so grateful to see his partner before. There wasn't a lot of conversation between the crime scene and the police station. Shelby had proven herself to be pretty observant, and there were things he would rather a five-year-old not hear. Plus, he didn't know how much Lissa could hear if he wasn't facing her. He didn't know that much about cochlear implants. His hypothesis was that with the implants, like hearing aids, the amount of benefit gained from the devices varied from one person to the next. However, Lissa seemed to hear most conversation. He wasn't sure how much lipreading she was doing, though.

When they arrived at the station, the two deputy marshals didn't take any chances with the safety of Lissa and Shelby. Parker walked in front of them, and Micah stayed behind them, each of them keeping one hand on his service weapon where he could pull it out instantly if any danger popped up.

Micah didn't relax until they were actually inside the Sutter Springs Police Department. Once they'd entered the main area, they were directed to the conference room. Chief Spencer met them there. The aroma of waffles, maple syrup, bacon and scrambled eggs hit his nose when the conference room door opened. His mouth watered.

It had been a long time since any of them had eaten.

"Waffles!" Shelby's joyful cry rang through the room.

Chief Spencer laughed. "Indeed. We had them brought in just for you, Shelby. Now, why don't you, your mother and the officers make yourselves plates."

"Sir?" Micah lifted his eyebrows questioningly. He'd expected to be briefed immediately. His stomach growled.

"It's okay, Deputy Marshal Bender." The chief placed a hand on his shoulder. "I know you're anxious to catch this killer. I am, too. He needs to be brought to justice. But you are going to need your strength. Fifteen minutes won't make a difference. We will talk soon."

Parker was already in line piling bacon on his plate. Lissa poured syrup on Shelby's waffles and cut them into inch-long squares. Shelby crunched on a slice of bacon while she waited for her mother to finish. The moment Lissa set the butter knife aside, Shelby tucked in, making no effort to disguise her enjoyment.

Micah couldn't stop the smile spreading across his face. Shelby was a gem. His gaze wandered over to her mother. The sun shining through the window sparked fiery highlights in her rich brown hair. He cleared his throat and averted his glance.

He couldn't get attached. There was no future in it.

She deserved someone who wasn't so broken. Someone who wasn't so haunted by his past. Until he'd gotten through those issues and made his peace with them, he wasn't a good fit for any woman.

His phone buzzed. Thumbing in his passcode, he read the information Marshal Hendrix had sent him.

The chief made good on his promise and gave them fifteen minutes to eat. Micah focused on his breakfast. He forked the last bite of scrambled eggs into his mouth, washed them down with a swig of piping hot black coffee, then set his silverware on his plate and pushed it away.

"I'm done," he announced to the room at large.

Parker laughed, shaking his head. Then he turned to Lissa. "I don't know if you've ever had a meal with Micah before. For some reason he always declares he's finished. I can't seem to break him of that habit."

Micah shrugged, unconcerned. He'd done that for his entire life. It didn't matter enough to change.

Chief Spencer smiled. "Well, now that Deputy Marshal Bender is done, I'll have someone come and take Shelby to another room so we can talk about what happened."

"Wait—" Lissa began to protest.

"It's all right." Micah reached out and covered her hand with his. "Lissa, Shelby will be fine."

When she looked at him with those large brown eyes, he felt like he'd been kicked in the chest. When was the last time someone had looked at him with that much trust? The weight of that trust was heavy on his shoulders, on his soul.

"I can assure you," Chief Spencer said, leaning forward, "your daughter will be safe. Lieutenant Bartlett will take her into the next room. I just don't think she should be in here for the conversation we need to have."

Lissa agreed, reluctance radiating from every line of her body. Several other officers entered the room, including Sergeant Steve Beck, Joss's husband. The two men shook hands briefly before Steve sat down.

Chief Spencer waited until the door had shut behind Lieutenant Bartlett and the little girl before straightening in his seat and opening the discussion that Micah had been dreading for the past hour.

"First, Lissa, let me say I am sorry for the loss of your friend. Tracy was a vibrant part of this department. We will not rest until her killer is found."

Lissa blinked rapidly but didn't speak. He wasn't sure if she could at the moment.

"I know this isn't easy, but we have to get our ducks in a row. Deputy Marshal Bender, why don't you bring us up to speed?"

The use of his full title gave an added sense of gravity to an already intense situation.

Micah stood and made his way to the front of the room. The air was thick with grief and tension. Tracy truly had been well loved in this community. He wished he could offer words of comfort.

But he couldn't. Tracy and Penny's murderer remained at large.

And Lissa was in his sights.

SIX

Lissa clasped her trembling fingers together in her lap as she prepared to listen to Micah's recitation of the facts. There was something horrific about the idea that Tracy's life could be rendered down to bullet points. She'd been more than a statistic on a serial killer's list. To Lissa, Tracy was irreplaceable. She didn't know if she would ever not miss her best friend.

She wouldn't cry. Her eyes burned with tears begging to be shed, but she refused to give in to the urge to howl her eyes out. Later when all this was behind her, she'd mourn. But not now. Now she would do her part to make sure this man, this evil killer, spent the rest of his life behind bars, where he belonged.

Micah looked so confident. She was beginning to know him a little better, though. She could see the stiffness of his shoulders. He was holding himself tightly in control.

He lost a fiancée to this killer. She couldn't even imagine that kind of pain. He had as many reasons as she did to want this murderer put away forever.

The conference room seemed smaller now that it teemed with members of the Sutter Springs Police Department. At least fifteen men and women, ranking from officer up to lieutenant, plus the chief, two deputy marshals and herself crowded into the room. There weren't enough chairs for everyone to sit. Many of the officers elected to stand along the walls.

"Eighteen months ago, on September fourth," Micah began, "Deputy Marshal Penny Adams was stabbed to death outside of her apartment. It was her thirty-second birthday."

Lissa glanced around the room. Recognition was stamped on every face. Just like Tracy, these men and women had known Penny. They also knew the man standing in front of the room had loved her. It had to be difficult, to stand there and methodically talk about her death as if she hadn't been the most important person in his life. She forced herself to listen, her hands clenched in her lap.

"The killer left a handmade birthday card near her body." He cleared his throat. "Six months ago, this past October, a second woman was murdered. Cassandra Phillips was an assistant district attorney in Cleveland. She was also killed on her birthday, and a card was left on the scene."

"Marshal," an officer interrupted, "was the second victim also stabbed?"

He shook his head. "She was strangled." He drew in a deep breath. She steeled herself for what she knew was coming. "As you know, Tracy Huber was bludgeoned to death yesterday."

She gasped, not having heard the manner of death before.

"So, he doesn't use the same method of killing?" one

of the officers clarified. "Is the birthday card the only similarity?"

"That and the fact that he kills them on or around their birthday. I have a theory."

The room grew silent, waiting. "I believe he's working on a calendar of sorts. That he's trying to find a victim who has a birthday in each month."

"So, are you saying he plans to murder nine more women?" another officer asked.

"Eight," Micah announced. An ominous silence pervaded the room while they waited for him to continue. "I talked with my superior an hour ago. Two months ago, Riley Sanders, a law student in Indianapolis, was shot and killed two days after her birthday, outside the library. The police arrested her boyfriend. But a few weeks ago, a passerby found the card, covered with blood. Yesterday the DNA results came back and confirmed the blood was Riley's."

The murders were coming closer together.

Parker spoke up. "We need to do a search and find out if there are any other murders that might follow this pattern."

One of the officers made a disgusted noise as he was tapping on his phone.

"What do you have, Steve?" Micah called out to him.

"Has anybody else looked at the news today? All of the major networks are talking about this perp, and you won't believe what they're calling him."

"Yes. I was getting to that," Micah remarked. "Obviously, there's another source talking to the press. It's my opinion the killer is the one responsible. Clearly, these theatrics are meant to gain attention. Although the press have not mentioned Riley yet. It's only a matter of time before they do make that connection. Anyway, they are calling him the Birthday Card Killer, or BCK."

Outraged chatter broke out in the room.

"I'm going to go out on a limb and guess that I'm not the only one that finds that really disturbing?" Parker said.

"There's more." Micah brought their attention back. "I know most of you have probably met Alyssa Page," he indicated her with his left hand. The officers all nodded. "The perp seems to have made her his next target."

"What?" Steve all but snarled. "He's going after another of our people?"

Shocked at his statement, she glanced around the room and saw them bristling. The looks sent her way shocked her. She might not be a cop, but these people acted like she was one of them.

"She cleaned the crime scene, Steve. He might have left evidence that could identify him, and thinks she saw it."

She had a thought, remembering an earlier conversation. "Micah, do you still think he'd consider a crime scene cleaner as someone in the same category as a cop, or a law student?"

Micah grew still. "Yeah. I think he probably would. Lissa, when's your birthday?"

If he was hoping her birthday would give them more time, she was about to disappoint him. She covered her mouth with her hand for a moment, trying to hold on to the control that was slipping away with each passing second.

Her belly quivered. Removing her hand, she answered his question. "My birthday is next week. Tuesday. May third."

* * *

Her birthday was only five days away. Less than a week to find a killer and keep her alive. Micah's pulse ramped up as this new information rushed through his mind. He'd thought he could hand her protective detail off to someone else, that he could walk away from her and relentlessly pursue the BCK. The name seared itself into his conscious. He could see the card, how it would look, the cake and block letters drawn as if by a child.

No. He ripped his focus away from there, not allowing his imagination to take it further. He hadn't known what was coming for Penny. There was no way, no foreshadowing or any hint that anything was wrong. But with Lissa, they knew the danger was lurking. He would be extra vigilant. He would keep Lissa and Shelby safe.

Chief Spencer put Parker in charge of a task force to gather information and see if they could discover any details that would lead them to the killer. Did the victims know the killer? How did the killer find them?

The chief went around the room, and he gave each person a task to concentrate on to assist the investigation. Finally, he came to Micah. Micah waited. It wasn't easy, but he knew that there could only be one person in charge. And as much as he wanted to be that person, it wasn't his call.

"Deputy Marshal Bender."

Micah had noticed that whenever he was talking with them professionally, Spencer always referred to the officers and marshals in the room by their full titles rather than by their names. It was probably his way of keeping things on track and reminding those he led that they were there to do a job. Growing up Amish, they'd never used titles like that. Micah didn't even address his aunts and uncles as *Aenti* Marta or *Oncle* Joseph. It was always by their first names, a reminder that all were equal in God's eyes.

It was one of the many changes he'd needed to get used to when he left the Amish culture. Now he barely noticed anymore.

"Deputy Marshal, I am putting you specifically in charge of taking Lissa and her daughter to a safe house and keeping watch there until I tell you otherwise."

Conflicting responses battled inside him, playing tug-of-war with his heart and mind. Micah had wanted to protect them, to see that Lissa, the woman who drew him like no other, and her little girl were safe, and nothing harmed them. However, he also had a stake in finding the killer and bringing him to justice.

"Micah," the chief broke out of his normal manner of addressing those under him and laid a comforting hand on Micah shoulder. "I know you want to assist. I know this is important to you, and I get why. But Lissa and Shelby need to be protected. It's my opinion that you are the person who is most suited to carrying out that duty. I'm literally putting their lives and safety in your hands."

He couldn't say no. Not when it was put in those terms. Micah nodded. He would do as the chief asked. In his gut, he knew he wouldn't be easy letting them go off with anyone else.

"Where do I take them?"

The chief frowned, scanning the remaining personnel as if what he was saying were top secret and he feared those in the room were listening. Then he motioned Micah outside. What on earth? Surely he didn't suspect any of his officers of not being loyal? The older man intercepted his glance before he could suppress his reaction.

"No, I don't distrust anyone under me," the chief said, a distinct bite to his tone. "I would trust each of these men and women with my life. That being said, someone is targeting us, and it looks like they are getting inside information, such as where people will be at any given moment. I need to have all the cars and homes checked for bugs."

Micah sighed, relieved that he wasn't the only one who felt there was a connection, more than occupational, to these murders. Someone who worked with or lived close to law enforcement might be the killer.

"That's a lot of suspects, Chief."

The chief nodded, and for a moment, his confident mask slipped to reveal a man who was weary and heartsore. But not defeated. Then the expression was gone. Micah half wondered if he'd imagined it.

"The fewer people who know about this place, the better. My brother bought a building, about an hour east from here." He described the location.

"I know the area. It's just twenty miles from where I grew up."

"I forgot about that. Well, anyway, it used to be an old schoolhouse. He thought it had charm and plans to make it into two apartments that he can rent out. He said the bottom apartment is done and he's already rented it out a couple of times."

"Is anyone living there now?"

"No. Bill fell off a ladder and broke his leg in two

places. He won't be doing anything construction-wise for another few months, and he won't let anyone else touch the project. I'm sure he'll let me use it for a safe house."

Within ten minutes, Micah joined Lissa and Shelby. Lieutenant Kathy Bartlett stood as he entered the room. "Ladies, I have enjoyed spending time with you. I need to go and get caught up. Lissa, you need anything, you have my number. Call me," she said.

To his surprise, Lissa stood and gave Kathy a quick hug. "I will, Kathy. Thank you for everything."

"You're welcome. You know how much Tracy meant to me."

Lissa turned to him. "Are we leaving?"

Her eyes were steady in her exhausted face. She was a rock. A surge of admiration swelled in his heart.

"We are. The chief has a safe place he's sending us."

"I'm sorry."

He blinked. That wasn't the reaction he'd expected. "Why?"

She bit her lip and shoved her hands in her pockets. Her head dropped. He waited until she lifted her chin and met his gaze. "I know you'd rather be out searching for the killer than babysitting us."

His hands shot out and landed on her shoulders. "Alyssa."

Her gaze widened, a bright blush sweeping her cheeks. Was she feeling the same connection he was? He ignored it, or he tried to. The attraction between them was not something he wanted to encourage. "I am doing everything in my power to stop the killer. Part of that, though, is keeping you and Shelby safe. It's not a burden. It's an honor."

She searched his expression for a moment before surrendering. Pulling away from his touch, she went to her daughter. He clasped his empty hands behind his back. They still tingled from touching her.

"Shelby, we've got to go. Okay? Marshal Micah is taking us somewhere."

Shelby grabbed her ever-present pony and stood. "Are we going home now, Mama? Sonny wants to go home."

That kid melted his heart. He wiped his mouth to hide a grin. At the same time, her plaintive plea made him want to scoop her in his arms and comfort her, like a father would his little girl. He pushed away the comparison.

"I'm sorry, Sweet Pea. We can't go home yet. Marshal Micah is trying to find the man who shot arrows at his car, so we'll be safe."

The little girl pouted, but she appeared too tired to argue. She reached for Lissa's hand. A phone started ringing. Lissa stopped and pulled her cell phone from her back pocket. She bit her lip.

"It's my boss." She unlocked the phone, but hesitated. "Should I answer it? I'm supposed to be working today."

"Go ahead and answer. Tell him you can't come in today, but don't tell him where you are."

"What if he fires me?"

Unfortunately, that was a real possibility, and not one he could do anything about. "I can't promise he won't. But it's not safe for you, or Shelby, to return to your normal routine. Not until this perp is out of the way."

She answered the call, putting it on speaker. "Hi Evan."

"Lissa! Are you all right, honey? Gage showed me a picture of your car. Is that a *wrecking ball*?"

She grimaced. "I didn't realize that made the news. Yeah, Some kind of fluke accident, right?"

"I've never seen anything like it. Are you all right?"

"Fine. I wasn't in the car. Listen, Evan, I'm going to be out of commission for a few days. I should have called you last night, but I got hurt at the scene and have a concussion."

Evan's voice shifted. "On the scene. Okay. Well, I need you to fill out some paperwork for the Occupational Safety and Health Administration. I'll send it to you. Get it back to me ASAP."

Micah stopped listening to the phone conversation and found several articles about the wrecking ball online. He sighed with relief when none of the newspapers reported a connection with the "Birthday Card Killer."

A knock on the door brought his attention around. Chief Spencer motioned for Micah to join him in the hall. Micah left Lissa and Shelby and closed the door behind him. Anyone who wanted to get to them would have to pass him and the chief. That wasn't going to happen, even if someone was bold enough to try to make a hit inside a police station.

"Slight hiccup in our plan, Deputy Marshal," the chief spoke in a low whisper. "My brother had let someone stay in the apartment, but only until tomorrow afternoon. We'll have to make other arrangements in the meantime."

Micah rubbed the back of his neck, sorting out what they knew in his mind. "Okay, look. I want to interview

Gage, the other cleaner who was on the scene. I think I'll have him come in and we'll do it here."

When the chief agreed, Micah ducked back into the room. He explained the issue to Lissa. "Do you have Gage's number?"

"Of course. Give me your number and I'll send his information to you."

Micah waited until she looked at him and then he recited his number. "Go ahead and save it in your contacts. Just in case you need it sometime."

She nodded, her fingers on the tiny keyboard.

"Out of curiosity," he asked her. "I was wondering in the car how much you could understand when a person talking isn't facing you."

"You know, I noticed that you always get my attention before you speak. I can hear you fine in the car as long as it's quiet. If there's a lot of background noise, then I might need to read lips. And sometimes, certain voices or accents are hard to make out. Your voice is deep enough I never have trouble hearing it. Shelby, though, I have to really focus on her when she talks."

"Good to know." His phone dinged. Her text with Gage's information came through. "I'm going to make this call, then I'll be back."

When he dialed the phone number she'd sent him, it rang five times before it was picked up. "Hey, this is Gage. I can't come to the phone right now, but you know what do! Leave me a message, and I'll call you back if I want to talk to you. Ciao."

Great. A message with an attitude. If he didn't really need to talk with Gage, Micah would have hung up without leaving a message. That wasn't an option, though.

"Gage, this is Deputy Marshal Micah Bender. I need to talk with you regarding a crime scene you worked on."

He rattled off his number, then disconnected.

He headed back to Lissa. When he opened the door, she shook her head at him, her eyes huge. She was on the phone. Pulling it away from her ear, she again pressed speakerphone.

"…you got to come over, Lissa. I don't know what to do. I need your help."

The attitude was gone, replaced by sheer panic, but he recognized the voice. Gage Wilson had reached out to Lissa. Why would he call her? He hadn't gotten the feeling that they were friends. In fact, he rather thought Gage irritated Lissa, but she tolerated him because they were colleagues.

She raised her eyebrows at him. He nodded.

"I'll be there, Gage. Stay put, okay?"

"Get here fast."

She disconnected and looked at him. "Why would he call you? I didn't think you two were close," Micah said.

"We're not." She shook her head and shrugged. "I can't explain it. He's never called me for anything not related to work. Although now that I think of it, I don't know that he really has anyone else."

"Not even Evan?"

"Evan's his boss. Not his buddy. I think he's even lower on Gage's list of people to call than I am."

"I'll drive you there."

"Shelby? I can't leave her here without me."

He made an executive decision. "We can't bring her to Wilson's house. Too dangerous. It might be a trap.

Call Ginger and I'll see if Chief Spencer can spare some police protection for the house while we're gone."

He didn't want to go to Gage Wilson's house. His goal was to get Lissa and Shelby to safety. But he couldn't ignore Gage's cry for help.

The man might lead them closer to finding the killer.

Or he might bring them straight into the killer's lair.

SEVEN

Lissa kissed Shelby for the third time at Ginger's front door.

"Relax, Lissa." Ginger nudged her over the threshold. "You go take care of whatever it is you and your hunky deputy marshal need to do. We'll be fine. How could we not? We have those officers over there to look out for us. And I will call or text hourly to let you know we're fine."

Heat seared her from her neck all the way to her widow's peak at Ginger's description of Micah. Granted, he was a handsome man. But he wasn't hers. Nor would he ever be. She'd learned her lesson with Teddy. She wouldn't put herself, or Shelby, in the uncomfortable, vulnerable position of risking rejection. Never again.

She ignored the edge of a grin threatening to explode across Micah's face. Of course, he'd heard Ginger. The woman didn't know how to whisper. Or she assumed that if she talked quieter, Lissa wouldn't hear her. Which might have been true, except she'd never had an issue hearing or understanding Ginger's speech previously.

Micah tapped her shoulder. "We need to go, Lissa. Before Gage panics and takes off."

She didn't like it, but she followed Micah to the car he'd managed to borrow. She wasn't sure who'd provided it, whether it was from the police, the US Marshals or merely a rental.

He opened the door and she settled herself in the seat. He folded himself into the driver's seat with a stoic face, his mouth barely turned down at the corner.

"Not exactly a vehicle built for someone your height, huh?" She couldn't help but chuckle at the scowl he threw her way.

He threw his arm over the seat and turned to back out of Ginger's driveway. When he turned around again, he chuckled. "I never realized how much I enjoyed the backup camera in my SUV. This one is, thankfully, only a short-time loan. Marshal Hendrix said my new vehicle will be delivered in a day or so."

"Hopefully, you'll return it in the same condition." She raised her eyebrows at him and smirked. "We do seem to be a little rough on cars."

The sound that left his mouth could only be described as a snicker.

They had to drive directly through the heart of town to get to Gage's house. If she remembered correctly, Gage had once told her he rented from a high school buddy. The house looked like it could've been a fraternity dorm. Both garage bays were wide open. One side was filled with sports equipment, tools and a motorcycle. The other side was relatively empty. The house itself could have used a layer of paint. Blinking against the sun, she glanced up near the roof. A few shingles had fallen off and the fascia boards showed in a couple of places.

"Let's get this over with." Micah opened his door and heaved himself out of the small car.

Lissa didn't wait for him to come and open her door. She was anxious to be done with this visit, too. She and Gage had never really hit it off, but she still found herself worried about him. Not for a moment did she believe he had anything to do with Tracy's death, or with the attacks on herself, but a bit of his fear seemed to have rubbed off on her. With every passing minute she was more on edge.

The rain had stopped while they were still at the police station. The sidewalk leading to the house was mostly dry, although there were a few puddles in some of the dips in the driveway. They walked up the three steps leading to the front door and Micah pushed the doorbell. He frowned.

"I didn't hear a doorbell ring. We'll give it a moment."

Lissa kept her fingernails against the railing while they waited. No one answered the door. "I think we should not."

Micah opened the screen door and rapped the wooden one with his knuckles. The door swung open.

"Whoa." He leaned into the house. "Gage Wilson? This is Deputy Marshal Micah Bender. I called you earlier. I'm here with Lissa Page."

No one answered.

"Should I try?" she asked.

"It couldn't hurt."

Lissa moved to the open door, conscious of Micah standing two inches from her. His presence eased her anxiety. "Gage? Can we come in?"

"He's not here."

They stepped back and looked at the young woman

with bright pink hair standing in the door of the other part of the duplex, chomping on a wad of neon pink bubble gum.

"Do you know where he is?" Lissa brushed her hair behind her ear. "I work with him. He called me an hour ago and asked me to come over."

The woman blew a bubble and popped it. She used her finger to shove it back into her mouth. "Nope. No idea. I saw his car drive off five minutes ago. Ten tops. He was driving fast."

That wasn't saying much. Gage always drove fast. He was always in a hurry or late. "That's not unusual," Lissa said.

Another bubble popped. "I know how he usually drives. This was extreme, even for him. It was like he was being chased."

"Did you notice anything else that seemed off?" Micah's arm brushed hers as he leaned toward the woman. He flashed his badge at her and introduced himself. "It's imperative that we speak with Gage as soon as possible."

The woman's teeth paused midchew. "Wow. I've never met a real-life marshal before."

Lissa didn't roll her eyes, but it was a close call.

The neighbor tapped her cheek with one impossibly long nail. "Now that you mention it, he had a duffel bag with him. He yelled something about a family emergency. I lived next to him for almost two years and I've never seen family visit him. In fact, he's never mentioned anyone."

Her words struck a chord with Lissa. Gage started working at the agency less than six months after she was hired. He'd immediately become a thorn in her side with his weak work ethic and flimsy excuses for arriving late and leaving early. Evan had turned a blind eye due to a lack of applicants. Not everyone could deal with the horrors they saw in their line of work. Gage had always appeared oblivious to the frustration of his colleagues. Inappropriate jokes, brash comments and overly graphic language commonly left his mouth, embarrassing those around him. He thought it was amusing to see Lissa blush with mortification. Despite this, no one had ever accused him of oversharing.

"He never talks about his personal life," she told Micah.

Gage's neighbor nodded vigorously, her pink hair bouncing with each movement.

Micah thanked the neighbor for her time and reached into the inside pocket of his jacket. He grabbed a stack of business cards held together with a rubber band and peeled off the rubbed band. "Here, if you see him, or think of anything else that might help us find him, we'd greatly appreciate it."

Lissa smiled at the young woman before pivoting on her heel, ready to walk back to the car and call Ginger. She needed to check on Shelby. So far, this errand had been a waste of time.

She took two steps before she heard the roar of an engine and Micah's shout.

"Get down!" His hands pressed her low to the ground. The neighbor landed beside her as a familiar white-and-black ATV with red trim hurtled around the corner.

Micah dropped in front of the women, his gun out of the holster and aiming. The ATV accelerated past them and zipped around their car. He couldn't shoot. There were people out in the front yard across the street, including children. If he missed his target and the bullet went wide, an innocent civilian could be injured or killed. When the driver reached the street, he slowed and held out a small remote control.

The house behind them exploded, sending Micah, Lissa and the neighbor off the porch and onto the grass.

Someone was screaming.

Micah forced his lids open. Smoke burned his throat and stung his eyes until they watered. He blinked several times to clear them. The air around him hung thick and hazy.

The house had exploded. The memory galvanized him into action. Springing to his feet, he swung around, taking in the extent of the damage. The family across the street clustered together. It must have been one of them he heard screaming. The father was talking on a phone. Hopefully, they'd called 911.

Lissa was on the ground three feet away from him. He met her eyes. She gave him a weak thumbs-up. She was fine.

The neighbor lady, however, lay beyond her. Lissa followed his gaze and gasped. She scrambled to her knees and crawled over to the woman. He strode over, but he already knew what he'd find. Her eyes were wide and staring. The blast had killed her.

Lissa felt for a pulse on her neck.

When she sat back on her heels, defeated, he squatted next to her and looped his arms around her shoulders. She half turned into his arms and buried her face in his shoulder. When her body began to shake, he tightened his hold.

"I never asked her name," she mumbled into his shirt. "If we hadn't come—"

He gently set her away from him so she could see his face. "I know. This isn't our fault. No matter who that perp was trying to kill, it's not our fault."

He had to remind himself as much as her. It was hard not to take responsibility for all the bad things that happened in his life. He was slowly learning that his perspective was skewed.

"Someone else is making these choices. We had no say in it."

"How do you move past things?" she sniffed.

He sighed. That was the question he had struggled with for years. "I haven't always. That's what led to me leaving my family. But I am realizing I have limited control over the events in my life. I have to rely on God. He's bigger than all the bad stuff. Otherwise, I'd have trouble getting out of bed in the morning."

She wiped her eyes. They were puffy, but clear. "Yeah, I get it, but the bad stuff still happens."

"It does. But God is there, even then. You never go through it alone."

He hoped that would provide some comfort. He snatched his phone from his pocket and called dispatch.

"911 has been called," Leslie, the dispatcher informed him.

"Thanks. We're going to need the coroner. A civilian was killed."

Leslie made the call.

"I need to talk with the witnesses," Micah told Lissa. "I don't want you sitting out in the open."

"I can't leave her alone." She pointed vaguely in the direction of the neighbor. Micah understood. He wouldn't leave her here unguarded. He stood next to her and bided his time. When help arrived in the form of his partner and a squad cruiser, he motioned Parker over and asked him to stay with Lissa while he talked with the bystanders.

"You sure? I don't mind doing the interviews." Parker tilted his head toward Lissa. Despite his attempt to play it cool, his partner had obviously discerned his growing attachment for the lovely brunette.

"I'm sure. I was here. It should be me."

And he needed to move, to help him get some mental and emotional clarity. The idea that Lissa could have died in the explosion overwhelmed him. His blood pumped fury from his heart to his head. He needed to move and be productive to burn off the anger mounting in his gut.

The neighbor, he learned, was a first-year art teacher at the high school. Desiree Neels. She wasn't married, but the mother in the house across the street believed she had a boyfriend. The cops planned to talk with him, but Micah was certain they'd find nothing more than a heartbroken man who had no connection to the explosion.

One more person the Birthday Card Killer had to pay for.

An hour later, he sat in the car next to Lissa as they headed to Ginger's house to get Shelby. He couldn't remember the last time he'd been this exhausted. Lissa's arms were crossed. Not in anger. She was shivering. The outside temperature had dropped. The air had a developed a little bite, and her jacket wasn't very warm. He flipped the heat dial to seventy.

"You have a heated seat. The control's there." He pointed her button, then hit his own, setting his heat level on high. She did the same. Soon, between the heated seats and the warm air flowing through the vents, he noted her shivers ceased. She uncrossed her arms and snuggled into her seat. Satisfied, he headed toward Ginger's house.

"What do you suppose happened to Gage?" she asked out of nowhere.

His thoughts had been running along the same vein. "I think this puts him at the top of the suspect list."

She shifted so she was sitting almost sideways and had a clear view of his face.

"Why would he blow up his own house?"

A curl distracted him. When he stopped at the stop sign, he paused and brushed it behind her ear. Her mouth dropped open in a startled O.

He flushed. What had come over him? "Sorry. Um, Gage. Well, he destroyed his house, but he also begged you specifically to come over. We didn't take that long to arrive. Only an hour. He didn't have to work today. According to everything the police could find on him, he had no family. He did have a sealed juvenile record, though. I want to check into that."

"Did he?" She sat up straighter. "I wonder if Evan knew that when he hired him."

"It was sealed. So maybe not." Thunder rumbled in the distance. A light rain splattered the windshield. Micah flipped on the wipers. "It's suspicious that he left with a duffel bag already packed when he knew you were coming, am I right?"

Silence greeted him. He shot her a glance. She nibbled on her thumbnail, her brow furrowed.

"Yes." She finally agreed. "When you put all the moving parts together, it does seem like he had an agenda."

"One more thing. He was the cleaner on scene with you at Tracy's house. How long did it take him to get there?"

Her head shot up and her mouth dropped open. "I remember! I'd forgotten arriving at the crime scene. I only beat him by a couple of minutes."

He was so shocked, he pulled over the car over to the side of the road and flipped on his hazard lights before turning to face her. "What do you remember? Exactly."

She rubbed her forehead as if massaging her head would bring the memories to the fore. "I don't remember much. I just recall arriving and seeing Kathy. She's the one who told me Tracy was murdered. I was waiting for Gage. When he showed up, a little after me, he didn't express any shock that Tracy was dead. I can't imagine that he didn't know who she was."

Newly energized by the prospect of having a suspect, Micah began making a list in his head of the next steps. He needed to get Gage's picture distributed. If possible, he wanted to see Gage's juvenile record. An interview with Gage's landlord, known associates and boss went on the list.

Until he was found, though, Lissa remained in danger. His failure to kill her tonight meant he couldn't stop targeting her. And if he believed he was under suspicion, the intensity of the attacks might increase.

Yes, Gage Wilson was looking very good for the murders. He had to find him, before Lissa became the next victim on his calendar kill list.

EIGHT

Lissa's head buzzed like she'd swallowed an entire beehive. Gage Wilson was trying to kill her. Gage. She shook her head, arguing with her own thoughts. It was impossible to reconcile the Gage she knew with the image of a man willing to murder random women.

Except they weren't random. He meticulously sought out women involved in one way or another with the legal system, and then he sorted them by their birthday months. How many women did he look at? And how did he choose the ones he killed?

Chills that had nothing to do with the cold strummed along her nerves and down her back. A thousand questions ran through her mind. She hardly knew what to ask first. Once Shelby was in the car with them, there'd be no more time for questions.

She sighed. It was getting late. The sun had begun its descent, and soon they'd have to find a place to stay for the night.

The chief's safe house wouldn't be ready until tomorrow.

"Where will we stay tonight?" she wondered out loud. "Do you think I should take Shelby to a hotel?"

"I don't." Micah responded. "You need a good night's sleep. I need to call the chief and see what he recommends. I need to talk with him, regardless, to ask about getting Gage's juvenile records released. That won't be easy. Many judges won't sign off on something like that."

"How important are those records?"

"If we see what led to his arrest then, it could lead to motive. Which could help us narrow the field of how exactly he chooses his victims. Any information we get helps. No matter how insignificant it seems."

She understood his point.

It was nearly six thirty by the time they arrived at Ginger's house. The sky was growing dim. The air smelled of puddles, wet grass and rain. They'd have another storm that night, for sure. She didn't want to go to an unfamiliar place to sleep. Exhaustion clouded her mind, and hunger made her legs feel weak.

Micah appeared at her side and surprised her by taking her elbow. "Here. You look done in."

"I'm ready to collapse," she agreed.

He waved at the cops sitting in the cruiser in front of the house. "I'm glad the chief is taking your safety so seriously."

"Yeah, me, too. Although I really hope the need for these extra steps is short-lived." She was anxious for her daughter to be a regular child again. Plus, every time Micah's arm brushed hers, she imagined she could see sparks flaring between them. She didn't want to be attracted to anyone. But it was more than attraction. She'd gotten a view of the man's heart and felt connected to him at some level. That was not at all what she needed in her life. Those things never ended well for her.

She knocked on the front door. Ginger opened it, then pulled her into a hug. She bit her lip to control her chaotic emotions. She'd probably cry herself to sleep, but for now, she didn't want to show weakness in front of Micah. Not again.

Shelby burst into the room and threw herself at her mother's legs. If Micah had not been standing at her back, the force of the little girl's weight smacking against her would have sent her reeling to the floor. His strong hand wrapped around her shoulders, securing her in place. Warmth filtered through her flannel shirt, driving off the chill she'd been feeling. Once she was steady, he removed his hands and stepped back. Immediately, she missed his warmth, his comfort.

Mentally, Lissa chided herself. She didn't need any man, no matter how safe they made her feel. She and her daughter were fine on their own.

"Mama! You were gone so long!"

It had only been several hours, but the past two days had been harrowing, so her daughter's exaggeration was warranted.

"I know, Sweet Pea. But I'm here now."

"And just in time to eat," Ginger announced.

Lissa sniffed the air. "Oh my. Do I smell your chicken and mozzarella casserole?"

"You know it. You'll have to help set the table."

"Done."

Ginger had inherited a box of recipes from her mother. Recipes handed down from one generation to the next, never to be shared with outsiders. It was considered a special treat when she broke out one of the prized dishes.

She could have served cold spaghetti and Lissa would have inhaled it, she was that hungry. But she'd never turn away her friend's excellent cooking. The small group ate with relish. Ginger, she could see, was dying to hear what they'd found, but the woman would never ask, and definitely not in front of Shelby's eager ears.

After they ate, she helped with the dishes. Micah joined her.

"Where do you think we should stay tonight?" she asked, rinsing off the last plate. "Is it safe enough to go home, do you think?"

He frowned. "I don't know. I'll have to talk to the chief."

"Why not stay here for the night?" Ginger interrupted them.

"Here?" Lissa blinked, startled. "I don't want to put you in danger, Ginger."

Ginger scoffed. "I'm the one with the security system, Lissa. I live conveniently close to the police department. I have extra beds. One of which is already holding your very soundly sleeping daughter. She's exhausted."

Micah tilted his head, thinking. "I'd have to see if the extra police could remain on duty. Between myself and both of them, we could handle taking shifts and checking the perimeter. Then tomorrow, we'll move out and see what the chief wants us to do. He's already disseminated Gage Wilson's picture, and we've described the ATV he's been driving."

Sheer exhaustion made her agree. Micah took out his phone and dialed. A few seconds later, she heard him talking to the chief. She wandered into the living room and sat on the couch while he talked. She'd ask about that conversation when it was done. The couch was more comfortable than she'd remembered. She leaned against the soft wing flaring out on the side, and lifted her feet, tucking them under herself. Her eyes drifted shut. The conversation behind her became white noise as she relaxed into a deep slumber.

Micah hung up the phone and sighed. Chief Spencer had agreed to let them stay at Ginger's for one night. The two officers on duty now would be relieved in one hour. Micah had planned to take a duty shift, but the chief had nixed that idea.

"Deputy Marshal, you will be taking full responsibility for Lissa and her daughter when tomorrow arrives. I'm still not completely satisfied that the danger to them is mitigated now that we have a suspect, no matter how promising this lead seems. Until it pans out, or we learn of a different lead, I still want to send you to a safer location. I also can't spare multiple cops for days in a row. We're a small department. Get some sleep."

"What about a warrant for his juvenile records?"

The crinkling of papers being shuffled came over the line. "I don't know how that will go. The judge you'd have to deal with for that is relatively new. I don't have a good read on him yet. We'll touch base at your earliest convenience tomorrow."

Micah agreed, silently vowing to be at the station when the a.m. shift started. He sent Parker a text, letting him know what was happening. His partner responded promptly, asking what he needed.

Micah started to text, then picked up the phone and dialed. Parker answered on the second ring. "Hey, Parker. Listen, can you see if you can run down the locations of the victims and Gage Wilson's alibi for each one?"

"I've already started on it. I'll have to do some legwork tomorrow, but I should be able to give you something solid by the end of the day."

That was what he wanted to hear. After ending the call, he walked out of the kitchen and stopped. Lissa was out like a light on the couch. Should he disturb her so she could go to bed? He hated to wake her up, but how well could she sleep propped up like that. She'd wake up with a crick in her neck for sure.

"If you can get her to wake up, I have a bed waiting for her." Ginger stood in the doorway. Her customary smile was gone, replaced by concern. "I don't know why anyone would want to hurt Lissa. She's kind to everyone."

"It doesn't make sense," he agreed. "If it makes you feel any better, I'm going to stick to her like glue until she's safe."

"I'm going to hold you to that promise, Marshal Bender."

Micah gently shook Lissa's shoulders. She blinked up at him, her expression soft and shy. A strand of hair got caught on her eyelashes. Without thought, he brushed it away. The soft skin of her cheek grew warm under his fingers.

He quickly removed his hand and stood.

Her relaxed expression vanished. Wide-awake, she slid off the couch and sidestepped him, making her way to Ginger. "Sorry, Ginger. I fell asleep on your couch. I'm more tired than I thought."

"You go to bed. I'll see you in the morning."

Lissa darted from the room without another glance at Micah. Ginger raised her brows at him. He flushed. He didn't normally make such personal mistakes. Never had he behaved so unprofessionally. Starting now, he would get his behavior under strict regulation. No more casual touches. He would keep his distance, at least emotionally, until she was safe and could return to her normal life.

And he would return to his.

Just a thought sent his spirits plummeting. He would miss her when they went their separate ways. For Lissa. She needed someone she could count on to be a good husband and father. Someone who wouldn't be so broken and hindered by past mistakes.

Someone who would give her what she needed and not fail.

He wished more than he could remember wishing for anything else, that he could be that person.

Sighing, he waited for the new security detail the chief had promised to begin. When the new officers arrived, he went out and made sure they knew what they were up against and what was expected of them.

Then, bone-weary, he went into the room Ginger had left ready for him and got ready for bed. Despite how exhausted he was, and even though the mattress pillow were probably the most comfortable he'd ever slept on, he couldn't turn off his mind. Over and over, he relived evading destructive arrows and almost getting killed by an exploding garage. Then he'd see Desiree Neels's vacant eyes staring into space. She didn't deserve to die like that. Neither had Tracy, nor any of the victims.

Finally, after tossing and turning for over an hour, Micah drifted into sleep, disturbed by nightmares where Penny and Lissa were both in danger.

He slept until 2 a.m., when he was suddenly awoken by bloodcurdling screams.

NINE

What was that? Had he dreamed he'd heard some-one scream?

Micah bolted up in bed. The room was pitch-dark, lacking even the faint light from the electric digital clock sitting on the small antique table beside his bed. He fumbled for his phone. It had a flashlight app on it. Unlocking it, he noted the battery was low and it wasn't charging. The power was out.

Micah didn't believe in coincidences. Especially when another shriek rent the air.

Footsteps pounded in the hallway.

He jumped from his bed and threw open his door. With his flashlight, he saw Ginger hurtling toward the back bedroom. The sound of breaking glass came from ahead of them. He increased his pace. Bursting into Lissa's room, he scanned the room for threats.

Ginger bustled in behind him. Lissa scrambled off the edge of the bed.

"There was a man trying to break in! He broke the window, then ran away suddenly. Shelby. I need to check on Shelby," Lissa gasped.

"Watch out for the broken glass!" Micah directed his light to the pile of glass littering the carpet in thousands of tiny shards. He didn't want her to cut her feet to ribbons.

She didn't respond. She was either ignoring him or hadn't taken the time to put her cochlear implants in yet. Given her concern for her little girl, he was sure it was the second reason. He dashed after her, anxious to reassure himself that Shelby was safe. When he entered her room, she was still asleep, her mother hovering near her side.

He walked over to Lissa and directed the flashlight toward his chin, hoping she'd be able to read his lips. "I need to go and check on the officers outside. This house should not have been breached."

"I understand. Why did we lose power? Was there a storm?"

He could hear the doubt in her voice.

"I'm still looking into that. I don't think it was an accident."

Ginger came further into the room and settled into the chair next to the bed. She handed something to Lissa. He waited to speak again until she had completed putting her implants on. Lissa carefully sat on the foot of the bed, scooting back until her back was against the wall. He wished he could see her face. He hated leaving her in the dark—literally in the dark—but knew he had to investigate what was going on.

He aimed the light at his face again, just in case she still needed to see his face. "Did you get a look at the man?"

"I can hear you fine, now, Micah. No. I didn't see

his face. He was in the shadows, but I think he was still wearing some sort of helmet."

"I think he probably heard us storming toward the room," Ginger offered.

"Yeah, probably." Micah stepped closer to the door. "Will you be all right if I go and check the perimeter? Do you have a cell phone you can call me with?"

Ginger waved her phone at him.

"We'll stay here," Lissa assured him. "I doubt he'll try to break in again now that we're all awake and watching for him."

He was counting on that.

Grabbing his gun, he headed for the front door, and slowly opened it. The cops on duty prowled around the edges of the house. Though he was relieved that they hadn't been injured, annoyance still burned in his gut that someone had gotten past them and breached the security system.

Glancing across the street, he exhaled between clenched teeth. The security light was on. Obviously, this was not a normal power outage. One of the officers jogged up to him.

"Marshal Bender."

"Yes, Sergeant."

"The electrical cable had been cut."

"I thought the lines were underground."

"Most of them, yes. But there are still some lines that are visible. Only three houses were affected."

Micah nodded. "He attempted to enter the house through the back window. One of the bedrooms."

The sergeant hissed. "He must have climbed over

the fence. It's just a chain-link fence. It wouldn't be difficult."

Assured that the cops were both alive and well, he headed back inside the house, his steps quickening as he approached the room. He was desperate to make sure the two women and the child were all in the same condition as when he'd left them. He didn't release the vise grip he had on his gun until he stood in the doorway and witnessed for himself that both Ginger and Lissa were fine. They'd found a couple of candles and had lit them, illuminating the room. The soft, flickering light danced over Lissa's face. He caught his breath. He had no business noticing how exceptionally pretty she was. But he did.

"You're back. Is everything all right?" she queried.

He cleared his throat, embarrassed to be caught staring. "Mostly. The cops are fine. They were already checking to see what had happened since only three houses lost power due to some lines being cut."

"What?" Both women gasped.

"Ginger—"

"It's okay, Lissa."

Micah stepped deeper into the room. "Actually, no, it's not okay. Ginger, I'm sorry. I have to take Lissa and Shelby somewhere safe. I don't want to leave you here, by yourself, while the perp is out there."

He didn't want to say it out loud, but if this perp became desperate, Ginger would be the perfect bait to bring Lissa out of hiding. If he needed to take her with him, he would.

"I've already thought of that." She wagged her phone. "I called my brother. Brian works the nightshift as a tow truck driver near Chicago, so he's awake right now. He told me I can come stay with him for as long as I need to. Since my job is online, I'll lock everything up and take my computer with me. No worries."

He sighed. That was one worry out of the way. "Great! Lissa, we'll stop by the station in the morning. The chief will have everything ready for us to go to a safe house by midafternoon."

"Should someone call my boss and tell him about Gage?"

"No. Right now, Gage is a suspect, but we're still open to other possibilities. I don't know how close your boss Evan and Gage are. I know you said that Gage saw him as just his boss, but right now, I can't run the risk of Gage knowing we're on to him. He might go into permanent hiding, and we'll lose him, or he'll escalate even more, trying to finish his deadly plan before we can catch him. I don't want him to hurt anyone else, not if we can stop him."

He didn't bother pretending to try and sleep any more. Adrenaline pumped through his blood. He went to the kitchen and used Ginger's Keurig to make some coffee, then sat at the table looking through the data Parker had sent him. Lissa brushed past him, leaving the scent of vanilla and cinnamon in her wake, and made herself some coffee. He watched her splash an absurd amount of pumpkin spice creamer into her mug before she placed it on the coffee machine.

"Are you sure you want coffee with your creamer?" he asked, raising his eyebrows and nodding toward her cup.

She wrinkled her nose at him. "Ha ha. I like coffee. I just like it sweet."

He gave a mock shudder.

A moment later, she joined him, a steaming mug smelling like a candle in her hands. He bit back a smile.

"Anything interesting?" She nodded at his phone.

"Maybe. Parker has been looking into Gage's alibis for the murders, and for the attacks on you. We know he was near the scene for your attack and Tracy's murder. He was at a conference in Indianapolis two months ago, when the law student was murdered."

"I remember that. There was some sort of Star Trek convention. He's really into science fiction."

"That still puts him near the scene of the crime. We don't know where he was when Penny was murdered. We do know he wasn't working that day. But that's all. Parker will keep searching and let us know the details as he finds them."

She took a small sip of her coffee. "I am still having trouble understanding how Gage can be a killer."

"Unfortunately, I've seen so many things I wish I hadn't in my life. People do some really dark things." He paused, questioning the sudden urge to share his private past with her. Very few people were aware of what had happened.

"What are you thinking?"

He closed his eyes briefly, then decided to let go. "You know I have a sister, right?"

She nodded. "Yes. Joss."

He cleared his throat. "When she was born, she was named Christina. She and Gideon are twins. When she was two years old, we were all out in our front yard, playing. My mother and my brothers and my sister. My mother stepped into the house to care for Gideon, who'd injured himself. I can't remember how. That's not important. Isaiah, Zeke and I were told to watch Christina. We were young. I was the oldest."

"How old?" she whispered.

"Eight." He swallowed a sip of coffee, dreading the next part of the story. "We were messing around, my brothers and I. When we looked over, Christina had wandered off. We looked everywhere. Someone had seen her and abducted her, planning to sell her. Of course, we didn't know this at the time. All we knew was she was gone and we were responsible."

Lissa's cup crashed on the table. She grabbed his hands in hers. He held on. "Micah."

"She was found twenty-two years later. The man who'd kidnapped her was arrested and is now in jail. And she's happy. The thing is, even though this horrible thing happened to her, and the man who abducted her had done so for nefarious reasons, my sister still grew up with God in her heart. God has a plan, even if people do bad things. I have to trust. But I still have a broken part of me inside that knows I failed my baby sister."

"Is she why you joined the Marshals?"

"I entered the army first. Spent four years doing that. I see plenty of bad. But I also get to see and do good in my life. I do believe God wants me to be a marshal."

"I'm glad you are, too. I can't tell you how much easier this is knowing I'm not dealing with it on my own."

She couldn't imagine the horror of knowing your sister was kidnapped while you were watching her. What a thing to put on a child! Lissa was glad Micah had found his place, but she also saw how honest he was being when he said he was broken. If he was broken by Joss's abduction, what had his fiancée's death done to him?

"Trust is hard," she admitted to him. "I try to trust God, but it's not easy."

"Tell me."

She bit her lip. But she wanted him to know she trusted him, too. "When I was in college, I fell in love and got pregnant. My boyfriend wanted no part of his daughter, and my mother said I was an embarrassment to my stepfather and kicked me out of the house. I didn't have enough money to pay for tuition, or for rent, and now I had a child to take care of. That's why I became a crime scene cleaner. It was an entry level position that paid well enough for me to make a living for me and Shelby."

"How old were you?"

"I'd just turned twenty. I became a Christian right after Shelby was born. It's funny, though. Jesus forgives us all our sins, but people don't. I walk into church, and there are still people who look at me like I don't deserve to be there."

"That's on them."

"True. But it bothers me that Shelby gets shunned. She's five. A couple of years ago, I met a man who I thought was my second chance at love. But Teddy's family convinced him that a 'fallen deaf woman' would only bring him down."

"I've never heard anything more ridiculous." He leaned forward. "You are lovely and smart. And Shelby is a treasure. You're better off without either of those men."

She nodded. "I agree. But it's really hard to trust people and their intention, you know?"

Ginger walked into the room, rubbing her eyes and breaking up the intense discussion. "If you two are up for the day, mind if I fix us something to eat?"

They dropped the topic and spoke of more mundane things. Three hours later, Shelby and Sonny joined them. Shelby was not impressed at the news they were leaving and not going home.

"It'll be an adventure, Sweet Pea."

The little girl thrust out her bottom lip and crossed her arms over her chest, still keeping a tight grip on the toy pony. She bit her lip when Micah hid a snicker with a fake cough. Her daughter was adorable, she had to admit.

"Does she ever set the pony down?" he mouthed.

"Rarely."

Shelby looked at her mother. "I don't want to have a venture. I want to go home."

It was a long morning. Shelby whined and moped around the house, dogging Lissa's every move. She tried to reason with Shelby, but five-year-olds weren't known for their ability to respond to logic. Normally, she'd hold her ground, but they had too much to accomplish in such a short time. Finally, she gave in and put in a pony movie for her daughter.

They ate a quick lunch, then she and Micah helped Ginger pack her car for her trip. She'd already cancelled her automatic grocery delivery which was to be dropped off later that day and rescheduled her hair appointment for the next week.

"If I need to stay gone longer, I'll reschedule again," she said when Lissa had worried about upsetting her entire life.

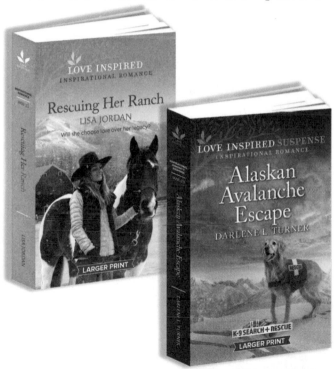

More to Love.
More to Explore.

With more to explore, we'd love to send you up to 4 BOOKS, absolutely FREE when you try the Harlequin Reader Service.

They say that "less is more" — but not when it comes to reading your favorite books!

We know that readers like you can't wait to open their newest book and settle down reading.

We feel the same way. That's why today, you can say "YES" to MORE of the great reading you love — absolutely FREE!

Try **Love Inspired® Romance Larger-Print** and get 2 books and fall in love with inspirational romances that take you on an uplifting journey of faith, forgiveness and hope.

Try **Love Inspired® Suspense Larger-Print** and get 2 books where courage and optimism unite in stories of faith and love in the face of danger.

Or **TRY BOTH** and get 2 books from each series!

Your free books are completely free, even the shipping! If you continue with your subscription, you can look forward to curated monthly shipments of brand-new books from your selected series, always at a discount off the cover price! Plus you can cancel any time.

So don't miss out, return your Free Books Claim Card today to get your Free books.

Pam Powers

Free Books Claim Card
Say "Yes" to More Books!

YES! I love reading, please send me more books from the series I'd like to explore and a free gift from each series I select.
Get MORE to read, MORE to love, MORE to explore!

Just write in "**YES**" on the dotted line below then select your series and return this Claim Card today and we'll send your free books & gift asap!

➡ *YES* ⬅

Which do you prefer?

☐ **Love Inspired®**
Romance
Larger-Print
122/322 IDL GRC6

☐ **Love Inspired®**
Suspense
Larger-Print
107/307 IDL GRC6

☐ **BOTH**
122/322 & 107/307
IDL GRDU

FIRST NAME   LAST NAME

ADDRESS

APT.#   CITY

STATE/PROV.   ZIP/POSTAL CODE

EMAIL ☐ Please check this box if you would like to receive newsletters and promotional emails from Harlequin Enterprises ULC and its affiliates. You can unsubscribe anytime.

LI/LIS-622-LR_MMM22

BUSINESS REPLY MAIL

FIRST-CLASS MAIL   PERMIT NO. 717   BUFFALO, NY

POSTAGE WILL BE PAID BY ADDRESSEE

HARLEQUIN READER SERVICE

PO BOX 1341

BUFFALO NY 14240-8571

NO POSTAGE
NECESSARY
IF MAILED
IN THE
UNITED STATES

Ginger had also checked with her neighbors and they had agreed to look out for any strange activity around her house. Lissa hugged her friend and said a quick prayer for a safe journey before joining Micah and Shelby in his short-time loan car.

Shelby was seated like royalty in the new booster seat Parker had brought by for her. She'd seen Micah casually slip him some money to pay for it. Apparently, that was one of the things he'd asked his partner to take care of. When she said she'd reimburse Micah, he'd waved her offer away.

"It's covered. The department will reimburse me since her seat was destroyed on our watch."

Hot tears sprang to her eyes. It had been a long time since she'd been the recipient of so much kindness. She'd gotten used to handling everything on her own because she'd assumed people wouldn't want to be bothered.

At the police station, the chief gave them the details and directions to the safe house. "No one here knows where you're going except for Parker and myself. Keep your phones charged and on you at all times. Deputy Marshal Bender, I want you to check in with me every four hours. Oh, and here are your keys."

He handed Micah two different keys.

Micah jingled them. "These aren't the same."

"That one is for the house." The chief pointed at the smaller key. "And that one—" he indicated the keyless fob "—is for the new SUV the Marshals office dropped off two hours ago."

Micah grinned, sending her pulse fluttering. She deliberately looked away before he could notice how flustered she was. It didn't matter how handsome he was, or how kind. She couldn't risk her heart, or her daughter's, by making the mistake of falling for someone again. If she needed a reminder, she'd recall the way Teddy's mother had looked at her. Micah might become fond of her, but that wasn't likely. Protecting her was his job. She wasn't the sort of woman he'd be bringing home to meet his parents.

She was silent as they moved their belongings from the rental to the new SUV, her heavy thoughts making it difficult to hold a conversation. She'd told him she was glad she wasn't alone, and she had meant it. But she still needed to prepare for his departure from her life. Because they never stayed.

"Micah!" They turned as Parker ran up to them. "Listen, buddy. I think we might have those records you wanted by tomorrow morning. The judge is considering your request. If I hear anything more, I'll let you know."

"Thanks, Parker. If we get them, hopefully, they'll help find him or figure out his next move."

If they found him, she could go back home to her life. Somehow, she didn't think she could return to her job. She'd never be able to walk into a murder crime scene again and stay objective. She'd always think of Tracy and know that whoever had died, they were someone's child, parent or friend.

"How do you keep doing your job?" she asked Micah. "I don't think I'll ever be able to do mine again ."

He set his computer bag in the hatchback of the SUV. "I think it's a grace. Being a deputy marshal, that's what I know. It's part of who I am. Even with all the harsh realities of the job, it gives me a feeling of purpose and satisfaction to know I'm making the world safer. But if I lost that feeling, or if I felt God wanted me to change careers, I'd do it in a heartbeat. If you need to search out something new, there's no shame in that."

He closed the hatch. "It's going to rain again. Let's get on our way."

No sooner had they gotten safely inside the car than the skies opened up again. She leaned forward in her seat to see the clouds rolling across the sky. They weren't ominous as if a thunderstorm were coming, but they were still hanging in the sky like wet bundles of misery waiting to ruin someone's day. She sighed. "I think it's rained every day this week."

He laughed softly. "Yeah, but it's spring. It's supposed to rain a lot. In August, do you say that it needs to rain because it hasn't rained all week?"

She laughed, too. "Guilty."

Micah drove away from the station, all his attention focused on driving. Silence reigned inside the car. It was a comfortable silence. He moved onto the main road in town. They stopped briefly at a stop light until it changed to green, then he began driving again. Lissa's thoughts drifted to her job and what she'd do when she got her life back.

She'd have to consider her options carefully. Whatever she decided to do, it had to take Shelby's schedule into account. She refused to let her daughter grow up without her mother being present. She already had no father in the house.

A thought occurred to her. "Micah. Do you realize tomorrow is May first?"

He glanced her way. "I've been thinking of that all day."

Yeah. She'd never gotten overly excited about her birthday. But this year, she had someone, possibly a colleague, hunting her down. If she got through this, she'd celebrate and appreciate each and every birthday she had from this day forward.

But first, she had to survive.

Shifting to glance out the window, she watched a green pickup truck moving through the late morning traffic behind them. The vehicle shifted into the passing lane, then back into the right lane, cutting it so close he cut off another driver.

"Someone's impatient," she commented.

Micah was already scrutinizing the rearview mirror. "I wonder. He's not stopping, even when people are honking at him."

She blinked and frowned. "Are many of the cars honking? I can't hear them."

He didn't answer. He moved his elbow from the windowsill, placing both hands securely on the steering wheel. His gaze flashed back to the mirror.

"Hold on."

Without any further warning, Micah spun the wheel and turned onto a side street.

Lissa shrieked and grabbed the handle. Swinging her head around, she swiped her hair from her eyes and watched as the truck she'd seen switching lanes careened after them. It wasn't an impatient driver.

They were under attack. Again.

TEN

Muttering a prayer under his breath that no pedestrians or children would decide to wander onto the street, Micah kept tabs on the fast-moving vehicle, which was gaining on them with every second. Neglecting to use his turn signal, he spun the wheel and zipped down another street. Three seconds later, the truck followed, running over the curb. This was no accident. Quickly dialing 911, he requested backup, biting off his coordinates so the police could clearly hear them. "Our tail is driving a green full-size pickup truck. The front grill is cracked, and the right headlight is busted out. I don't know the make and model. I can see one person in the cab, but he's wearing a helmet of some kind. I can't see any other identifying features."

"Two units are on the way, Marshal Bender. They'll intercept you within the next few minutes."

If they had a few more minutes.

The truck roared closer. The bumper nudged his SUV. He held on to the steering wheel, managing to keep the SUV on his side of the street.

Micah turned again, striking the curb with the front

tire. He winced but kept going. A bruised tire was better than what that driver had planned. Veering close again, the truck struck them hard enough to cause the SUV to swerve. Micah regained control, sweat gathering on his collar. He blocked Shelby's cries out, focusing on getting them to safety.

This time, the truck struck them so hard, Micah's vehicle jumped the curb completely and he found himself driving down the center of someone's lush green lawn, the tires cutting up the wet surface and leaving ruts. The truck followed after them.

"Look out!" Lissa screamed.

Looking up, he watched the barrel of a gun emerge from the window. He clenched his jaw so hard it ached, then swerved hard, his tires spitting grass and mud, and spun around, facing his opponent. The other vehicle shifted into Reverse and took off. Micah left the grass and drove back onto the paved road. The vehicle bounced funny.

Frustrated, he slapped the wheel. They weren't in any shape to chase anyone, not with a flat tire.

By the time backup arrived, the other vehicle was long gone. Micah and Lissa got out and changed the tire, leaving both of them hot, tired and filthy by the time they hopped back into the car. And cranky.

Micah plugged in his phone again and headed out.

"Lissa, keep watch for that truck. I want to know if any green vehicles pop up on your radar." None did. The rest of the trip was remarkably uneventful. He turned onto the driveway of the safe house, half an hour later.

He would have never found this place without his GPS. That was one benefit of this place.

Micah cut the engine at the back door. That was another plus. His vehicle wouldn't be visible on the road. Nor could people see the house, or them, if they were driving by. Unless one knew the area, in fact, it would be possible to pass by this house without even knowing it was there. Altogether, the perfect place to hide from a killer.

At least he hoped it was. He pushed the button to open the hatch, then got out of the vehicle and stretched. The long night was catching up with him. Judging by Lissa's wan expression, she was feeling their early morning wake-up call, as well. If all went smoothly, they'd go to sleep early tonight.

"Wait here," he told Lissa. She took her hand off the door handle. "I know the chief said no one knows about this place. I need to make sure it's secure, though."

She nodded her agreement. "Go. We'll be here when you're done."

Micah made his way up the little walk to the back door. The walk was still damp from the recent rain. The back porch was dry, situated under an awning. It looked freshly swept, too. The chief had said his brother had let friends use the place for the past couple of nights. Micah had questioned him about these guests. After all, Chief Spencer assured them no one knew about the place.

"No one from the station knows about it," he'd clarified. "As I told you before, my brother bought this building to turn it into apartments he could rent. When he got injured, he said I could use it. But he'd forgotten that he'd already agreed to let a group of writers from out of state hold a writing retreat in the downstairs apartment. They left this morning."

Not anyone who'd know about what was going on with their investigation. Micah was suspicious by nature, but he had to let it go at that.

Using the key, he unlocked the back door and let himself into the house. It was scrupulously clean. The writers had left no trace of their retreat. Those are the kinds of guests he appreciated. The garbage cans were empty, even.

Cautious, he made his way upstairs to make sure no one was hiding there. Signs of construction were everywhere. Tools, paint supplies, and drywall were stacked along the walls. He peered around every corner, searching for any unwelcome guests. Five minutes later, he sighed and relaxed his shoulders. All clear.

Returning his gun to its holster, he headed down the stairs to go back outside. A sharp cry interrupted his musing. Jumping over the remaining steps, he dashed outside, tearing his gun out again.

A person wearing a helmet was trying to pull Lissa from the car. She was fighting him for all she was worth. Inside the car, Shelby screamed, terror in every cry. He thought he recognized the helmet from the driver of the green truck, who seemed much shorter than he'd imagined, though.

"Stop! US marshal!" The attacker shoved Lissa away and pulled out a gun. Using both hands, the figure aimed at Micah, finger on the trigger.

Lissa sat sideways on her seat and slammed both feet into him, her boots solidly connecting with his hip. His shot went wide, the bullet lodging in the wall of the house behind Micah. Micah charged at him before he could catch his balance, knocked the gun from his hands and had the shooter up against the side of the vehicle, legs spread, within ten seconds. Lissa pulled her legs back inside the vehicle. Micah heard her comforting Shelby while he cuffed the would-be kidnapper.

"Is that him?" Lissa's voice asked him. At least she'd waited until the guy was cuffed before leaving the vehicle. "Is that the man trying to kill me?"

Immediately the helmeted head shook wildly back and forth. "Wait! I didn't come here to kill her!"

It was a woman's voice.

Micah removed the helmet. The woman, really little more than a girl, stared at them, her blue eyes huge and frantic in a bloodless face.

"Really?" Micah mocked, masking his own surprise. "You shot at me. That looked like you were trying to kill someone."

She shook her head again. "No, I'm trying to earn some money. That's all."

He wanted to ask her more, but any information he got before he read her rights wouldn't stand up in court. Regardless of why she did it, no matter how pathetic her story was, she'd been willing to use deadly force to kidnap Lissa, endangering a child, and had pulled a loaded gun on a deputy US marshal. She was on her way to prison, no doubt about it.

"Lissa, you two go into the house and lock the doors. I will call this in."

Lissa hopped from the vehicle and sprung Shelby from the booster seat. Grabbing her daughter's hand, she rushed past Micah, taking the key from him as she went by, and disappeared into the cabin. The lock snapped into place behind her.

He sat the would-be kidnapper into his car and stepped away from her, using his cell phone to call for backup. When he hung up, he surveyed the scared woman in the SUV, running a hand over his head, stopping to rub his neck. He needed coffee. He also needed to figure out how the killer kept finding them. There had to be some kind of trace on them. Maybe a tracking device. The chief had said he was going to have all the cars and homes checked for bugs. Had he done it?

Getting back on the phone, he had the chief on the line in seconds and explained what had happened.

"Chief Spencer, did the homes and vehicles of all personnel get checked for bugs?"

The chief's answer was swift. "They did. We checked the precinct, too. I don't know how they found you, Micah. I apologize."

Micah didn't know, either. "They knew we were coming here. She waited until—"

"She?" the chief exclaimed. "I thought we were after Gage Wilson."

"We still are. This was not the same person who shot arrows at us. I'm positive. She's much smaller than the person we'd seen before. She struggled to get Lissa out of the car. And they're about the same height. Lissa might even be an inch or so taller. I don't see this person able to hold that lead crystal vase high enough to hit Lissa's head where she did. Nor do I think she could overcome a trained officer in a frontal attack."

When the police arrived to take over, he left them to go and check on Lissa and Shelby inside the house.

When he entered, the scent of waffles met him. He followed his nose into the small kitchen area. Shelby was at the table, her mouth full, a smudge of maple syrup on her left cheek.

Titling his head, he gave Lissa his best "What's going on?" look.

She shrugged. The toaster dinged, and two more waffles popped up. "Want these?"

"No, thanks. I have to go back out there. I wanted to make sure you two are okay."

"We're fine. Shelby needed a distraction. Waffles always work. I was glad to find these in the freezer." She put them on a plate. "Do we know why she tried to kidnap me?"

"Not yet. I believe her story, that she was paid to take you, but where? And who paid her?"

"Are you still thinking Gage is behind everything?"

"I am." He hesitated, glanced at Shelby, who was intent on attacking her food. He hated to bring disappointing news, especially now that Shelby had calmed down and seemed to be accepting their present circumstance. But he wouldn't lie to her. Not ever. That wasn't his style. He preferred to have no surprises. "You know we're not staying here."

"I figured. How are they finding us?"

He leaned against the counter and watched Shelby pretend to feed Sonny a bite. He had to grin. She sure was a cute little thing. "I haven't discovered that yet. The chief said they'd searched for bugs on their end." He straightened. "My vehicle is new. I'll check, but I doubt there's anything on it."

"You'll find out how. I have faith in you." She poured

syrup over her own waffles and took a bite. "The chief's brother has a Keurig."

He grinned. "That I won't turn down."

He made his way to the coffee maker and found a deep roast pod and a large mug. Soon the aroma of coffee had blended with the scent of the waffles. He sniffed again. "I got to get back out there."

The waffles looked good, though. He paused near her. He didn't have time.

"Here." She held up her fork, a large slice of waffle dangled from it, the syrup lightly drizzled on top. "You can have the last bite of this one."

He gave in to temptation and bent down to take the bite. Their noses nearly touched. He stood up swiftly, his pulse hammering. "Thanks."

Had he come close to kissing her? She held her hand over her heart, trying to get her breath back. It wasn't even 10 a.m., and they'd had an exciting morning already, even without the almost kiss that had knocked her off balance.

Her mind returned to the matter of how the killer kept finding them. This house was literally out in the boonies. It was so far off the main roads they probably couldn't even get cable lines here. So how did they know? If his car wasn't bugged, and the station wasn't—

They'd never checked her stuff. She'd been carrying that pink camouflage backpack with her since this started. It had been in the trunk of her car before she'd gone to Tracy's house.

She ran to the door of the house. "Micah!"

He came running. "What's wrong? Is everything all right? Where's Shelby?"

She put a hand on his arm to calm his panicked questions. She'd not seen him this flustered before. His concern warmed her heart. She shoved the warmth away. There was no time to let herself get bogged down with emotions.

"Everything's fine. But I think I know how they're finding us."

That got his attention. "I'm listening."

"I think whatever they're using to track us is in my bag. The one I had in my trunk."

He lost color, shocking her. "Of course. Where is it?"

Spinning, she ran over to the bag. She'd brought it in with her to charge her batteries while he'd dealt with the attacker. Her neck tingled when he came to stand behind her. Fingers trembling, she shoved the bag into his waiting hands.

Micah upended the bag over the overstuffed couch in the living room. The contents spilled onto the plush cushions. She and Micah went over each item that had been in her bag. Nothing. Then he looked up at her.

"What about Sonny?"

A chill swept through her. The toy went everywhere they went, too. The idea of someone, a killer, getting that close to her daughter, had the acid pooling and roiling in the pit of her stomach.

She walked to her daughter. "Honey, we need to see Sonny for just a minute, okay?"

She held out her hand. Her daughter gave her the pony. Lissa marched back to Micah and handed the animal to him. Feeling her legs wouldn't support her, she dropped down on the matching living room chair, watching his every action. He squeezed and examined each inch of the pony.

"I can't feel anything." He whispered to her. "Before we take the horse apart to search more thoroughly, did you remove everything from the bag? Is there anything at all left in here?"

"My charger."

Standing, she moved to the counter in the kitchen and grabbed her cochlear implant battery charging dock and the cord. She removed the batteries. He'd never realized how big they were. Each one was nearly an inch long. He checked each one, then handed them to her. Next, he flipped the charger over. There was a silver sticker on the bottom. A sticker that described where the device was made. She'd not paid any attention to it. He ripped off the sticker. A small square object stuck to the bottom of it.

"That's it."

Her jaw dropped.

"How long have you had this charger?"

She shook her head. "I don't know. Six months. Maybe seven."

He handed the charger back to her. "So, either he just did this on Wednesday after he attacked you. Or..."

"Or?" she prompted, impatient when he hesitated. "Or what?"

He bit out the next words as if they caused him physical pain. "Or he was planning for you to be his next victim all along."

She stumbled back, hitting the wall. Her legs gave out. She slid down until she sat on the floor. She'd been targeted for months. Had Gage been watching her for all this time, taking note of her patterns?

"That's how he knew I'd take Shelby to Ginger's. It wasn't uncommon for us to bunk there if I finished late at night."

He nodded, his face mirroring his concern. "He'd know your car. Have you ever handed him your keys?"

"Yes. We've both been in each other's cars. Same with the other cleaners. Sometimes equipment is in the car, and you need someone to go and get it. Or it's too much to carry alone, so you ask for help. It's all part of the job." She had never questioned it. When Gage had asked for the keys, she'd throw them to him without hesitation.

She'd trusted him, at least at work, enough to let him have access to her private space. "My bag was always stuffed in the corner of the trunk. I never thought it looked like someone had tampered with it."

"Why would you? He was your colleague, even if you weren't friends. He'd have no reason to get into your bag. Your actions were natural. His were the reprehensible ones."

"Maybe. But my trusting my coworker has led to my daughter being put in harm's way."

Footsteps clomped across the porch. Micah gave her a last look, then opened the door and let the police officer in.

"We're taking the woman into custody. She wants to talk with you, Deputy Marshal."

Micah nodded. "I'll be right there."

He waited until the officer had left before turning

back to Lissa. She saw the determined glare he aimed at her.

"We're going to get him, Lissa. No matter what it takes, I will put this killer behind bars so you and Shelby, and all his other prospective victims, will be safe."

He walked out the door. She sighed. He meant what he said, she could tell. He really would do everything he could to protect them.

But she knew he couldn't promise to keep them safe. This cat and mouse game they were playing with the killer reminded her of a high school wrestling match. No matter how many points you had, if your opponent took you down for a pin, you were done.

There was only one winner.

ELEVEN

Micah found, oddly enough, that he didn't want to talk with the woman who'd nearly run them off the road earlier. She'd tried to shoot them, then attempted to force Lissa from the SUV. He was more than a little confused, too. Why didn't she shoot Lissa instead of grabbing her?

Folding his arms across his chest, he growled down at the subdued woman. "I hear you want to talk with me."

"I do." She bobbed her head. "Look, I didn't try to kill you—"

"You shot at us."

"No! I mean, yes, I did, but I shot at your tires. I was hired to kidnap the brunette with you. Not kill her."

He frowned, tightening his hands into fists to control the fury mounting inside him. "Were you read your rights?"

"Look, I know I don't have to talk, but I want a deal."

"That depends on you. If I like what you tell me, I'll be willing to negotiate. But if you don't cooperate, I won't go easy on you." He leaned closer. "I want to know who hired you."

"I don't know! Honestly!"

Fed up, he pivoted and returned to the house, dialing Parker's number while he walked.

"Parker here."

"Hey. There's a woman coming to the station. She's under arrest for attempted murder, attempted kidnapping, and endangering a minor. She claims she doesn't know who hired her. I'm not buying it, but on the off chance she's telling the truth, see if she can identify our suspect."

"Will do."

"I'm also going to send in a tracking chip we found on Lissa's charging device. See what information you can find there."

"On her device?" Parker exclaimed. "Are you kidding me? How would something like that even get there?"

"No idea. My guess is this guy had her in his sights long before now."

There was a brief silence on the other end. "Micah, how well do you know Lissa? Is it possible that she's working with the killer? Could she have given him information on Tracy, and is trying to cover her tracks? Is that a possibility?"

"Parker, trust me. She is not involved. There is no way Lissa would risk her daughter's life. And don't forget, she was nearly killed. You don't bash someone on the head with a lead crystal vase and not know they could die."

"I guess. Look, dude, I'm sorry. I can hear I've upset you. I'm trying to be logical here and think of all the angles."

"That's not one of them."

"Fine. I'll drop it. I believe you."

Micah continued walking.

"Where are you going to go next?"

Micah had an idea. He opened his mouth to tell his partner, then snapped it closed. "Better you don't know for the time being."

"You're not going to tell me? That's nonsense. Micah, I'm your partner."

"You are, and I'd trust you with my life. I've done it in the past. But this time is different. Somehow, the information about our whereabouts has been getting out. I'm almost positive that getting rid of the tracking device will solve this problem. But just in case it doesn't, I'm going off the grid for a bit. I'll call in when I can."

Parker argued with him, as he knew he would. If the tables had been turned, he would've argued. He would've done everything he could think of to change his partner's mind. Going off on your own was never a good idea. That was why the deputy marshals worked in pairs. This time, though, he needed to do things differently. Until he knew exactly how the killer was getting his information, he was going solo.

Less than five minutes after he hung up with his partner, Marshal Hendrix called him. He'd been expecting this.

"What's this I hear about you going off on your own? You know that's not how we do things here."

As patiently as he could, Micah explained what he had planned and why. He didn't tell his boss where he was going, but he told him all the incidents that had led up to his decision.

"I don't like it, Micah. It sounds dangerous and reckless. If any other deputy had come to me with this plan, I would have nixed it immediately."

Micah perked up. He heard a "but" in there somewhere. He could hear it in his boss's voice. He didn't interrupt, waiting for his boss to come to a decision. He held his breath, praying Marshal Hendrix wouldn't say no. He'd hate to go against a superior officer's orders, but he had promised Lissa he'd keep her and Shelby safe. That was more important than any job.

"I'm going to allow this, just this once, Deputy Marshal Bender. On three conditions."

Micah tightened his grip on his phone. "Yes, sir?"

"The first condition is you have to continue to call in to me, every four hours. Go get yourself a cheap burner phone, if you need to. I'm going to give you a different phone number, one only used in emergencies."

Micah got out the small notebook he carried in his pocket and a pen. He could have used his phone, but he had never trusted technology. This worked just as well. He copied down the number Marshal Hendrix rattled off. He'd need to memorize the number as soon as he got off the phone and burn the paper so no one else would get their hands on it.

"I got it. That's one condition."

"Good. The second condition is that I want to know immediately about any changes in your circumstances."

He understood what the marshal was saying. If they got hurt, or if he caught Gage. Or if they were ambushed again. He could do that.

"Got it. That's two."

"Right. The third condition, Micah, is I need your head one hundred percent in this. You're protecting two assets... Alyssa Page and her daughter. If you find you can't separate what's happening now with what happened eighteen months ago, you need to let me know and we'll make other plans."

"I can do this, sir. I will abide by those conditions."

"Great. Call me as soon as you have the burner phone. Tell no one else, not even Parker. I don't want anyone else to know what we're doing here."

Micah disconnected the call and jogged up the stairs. Despite the chill in the air outside, the inside of the house was warm and cozy. It also smelled like chocolate chip cookies. Did Lissa's house always smell this delicious? Strolling into the kitchen, he grinned. Shelby was standing on a chair next to the counter, her little tongue poking out of the side of her mouth while she stirred a bowl filled with cookie dough. Lumps of the same dough dotted the floor and the cupboard, and there was a large clump in her mother's hair.

"What's this?"

"Marshal Micah!" Shelby flashed him her heart-stopping smile. "Mama and me is baking you cookies. Cuz you saved us from the bad person."

His eyebrows climbed his forehead. His neck grew warm. He couldn't remember the last time someone other than his mother had made him cookies.

Lissa chuckled. "She needed something to do. This worked. The chief's brother keeps a well-stocked inventory. We had everything we needed, and we can take them with us when we—" she gave her daughter a quick glance "—L-E-A-V-E."

He chuckled, quickly bringing his fist to his mouth and changing the laugh into a cough. "Are we spelling to keep someone from understanding what we're talking about? Wouldn't it be better to say what we mean so she won't be shocked?"

She ran her hands through her hair, grimacing when they encountered the blob of cookie dough. She dug her fingers into her hair and yanked it out. "Yuck."

"You missed some." Leaning over, he reached one hand out and sifted it through her silky dark brown hair, dislodging the remainder of the sticky dough. His eyes never left hers as he plopped the chunk in the trash can. Electricity simmered, the air between them nearly vibrating with it. Without thinking, he lifted his hand again and touched her flushed cheek. The skin warmed further under his fingertips.

She was so beautiful, inside and out, she took his breath away.

Lissa couldn't breathe. The sensation of his hand against her skin, the yearning blooming in his gaze, caught her like a fly in a spider's web. She was powerless to glance away or step back. At this point, it was hard to remember why she wanted to.

"Mama! Do the cookies go in the oven now?"

Shaking her head to clear it, she laughed, her voice shaking. She nearly leaped away from Micah. Her heart pounded in her chest. What had she been thinking? What if he'd tried to kiss her? It terrified her to admit, she would have allowed it. She had wanted him to kiss her.

This wasn't good.

"Yes, Sweet Pea. We need to put these in the oven." Her hands trembled as she slipped the neon yellow oven mitts over her fingers. Deliberately, she avoided Micah's gaze while she set the timer for ten minutes. "You'll have to listen for the timer, Shelby."

"I know, Mama. You can't hear it."

"Exactly." She could use her phone. It would vibrate. But she was charging it and didn't want to use it unnecessarily. It was obvious they'd soon be on the move, and she didn't have a car charger with her. She couldn't use Micah's. They didn't have the same sort of cord. Her phone was much older.

She happened to glance at him, then wished she hadn't. His intense gaze watched her. Flushing, she jerked her face away, letting her hair swing forward so he couldn't see it.

When he walked away from them, she leaned against the kitchen wall, nearly limp with a mixture of relief and regret.

By the time the cookies were all baked and had cooled, she'd calmed down. Lissa chided herself for acting immature. She wasn't a teenager on her first date. She was an adult woman with a child. And Micah wasn't her boyfriend. He was a man sent to protect her from a killer. End of story. He was probably looking forward to closing this case so he could move on with his life, too.

Lissa packed the cookies into baggies. When she moved out to the main living area, Micah already had everything packed up and ready to go. Lissa noticed that Shelby was pouting again.

"You told her we're leaving?"

He nodded.

"Mama. He said the bad people are still after us and

we need to find somewhere safe." She hugged Sonny closer to her chest.

Lissa struggle for a moment. Part of her wanted to be mad at him. She was the parent. Shouldn't it be she that decided when and how to break the news? The other part, though, recognized that Shelby needed to know. It was going to happen whether she had a meltdown or not, and the child was better off being prepared.

She knelt down in front of her daughter, brushing her hair away from her sweet face. Her baby was growing up so fast. If only she could keep her ignorant of the evil in the world. But it wasn't possible, and sometimes sheltering too much was detrimental to the child's ability to heal and make good decisions. "It's true, honey. We need to go again. I need you to be brave. I know it's scary, but I need you to not cry and to be quiet when we leave, can you do that?"

The child nodded, tears welling and clinging to her dark lashes. "I'm scared, Mama."

Lissa took her baby in her arms. "I'm here. And so is Marshal Micah." She set her child back. "And God is looking over us, even though we can't see Him."

With less attitude than she'd previously shown when they moved, Shelby allowed her mother to buckle her into her booster seat. Lissa kissed her, letting her lips linger for a moment, praying for her daughter's safety and that God would protect them all as they traveled.

Micah had yet to say where they were going. Frustration grew as he continued to prepare for the journey, silently. He didn't appear angry. Decisive. That was the word. Each movement was made for a purpose.

The sky rumbled. In the distance, flashes of lightning

parted the sky. Micah drove away from Sutter Springs. This time, he didn't have the map app open on his phone. Wherever they were headed, Micah apparently knew how to get there.

"My partner said something that really upset me today." He finally broke the silence.

"I'm sorry. What did he say?"

He flashed her a quick gauging glance. "You won't like it."

"Well, now you have to tell me."

"Yeah." He hit the switch for the wipers when fat drops hit the windshield. "He suggested that maybe you were the link and were helping the killer by leading us astray."

Her mouth dropped open. "I would never—" She couldn't form the words to describe her feelings. She realized she'd started to yell and sucked in a deep breath to calm herself.

"I know you didn't. I told him that."

Her neck and shoulder muscles relaxed when she realized he'd defended her against his partner, whom he'd known and trusted much longer. "Thank you."

"You're welcome." He smiled briefly. "It did get me thinking, though. We know that you did have a tracker on you. While you were making the cookies, I checked your stuff again. And I checked S-O-N-N-Y closer."

When she glanced at him, she got a wink for her trouble. She chuckled at his attempt to tease her about spelling out words earlier, but it was a half-hearted laugh. She couldn't remember feeling so discouraged. Tracy's killer had stolen her orderly life, too.

"I'm assuming you didn't find any more trackers."

"You are correct. But I am still concerned about how easily we've been found. I called my boss. He agreed that for the time being, we're going rogue."

That sounded extreme. She tilted her head and regarded him, searching for any signs of joking. When she didn't see any, she sighed. "I already don't like this plan. Give me the details, please."

Glancing in the mirror at Shelby first to make sure she wasn't listening, he repeated his conversation with his boss, Marshal Hendrix.

"Where are we going, though? If we can't let anyone know, will we hide in a hotel?"

"Nope. We're going to do something radical. It's going to be difficult, but we're going to go stay with my family. We're going to hide with the Amish."

TWELVE

Lissa's mouth dropped open and she stared at Micah, sure she'd heard wrong. "Stay with the Amish? We can't live that way."

He frowned at her, his expression faintly offended. "Of course, we can. I lived that way for nearly eighteen years. It's a hard life, but there's nothing wrong with it."

"Micah, have you forgotten something? I'm deaf."

At his confused expression, she pointed to her implants. "I rely on electricity to charge these. Without them, I'm deaf, and I don't know any sign language. I can lip-read, but it's exhausting to rely on it for communication."

She twisted her fingers. He reached over and dropped one hand on top of hers, stopping the nervous motion. "You don't need to worry. While it's true that some communities don't allow any electricity or batteries, the bishop in my parents' district is more lenient. He allows for things like hearing aid batteries and cochlear implant chargers. There's a couple of people in the district with implants. I've never met them since I'm no longer part of the district, but my parents and brothers have talked about them. The bishop also allows for small rechargeable battery-operated charging equipment. At night, it's used to charge the implants, then during the day, the battery pack itself is charged at the family business. We can all have electricity in our businesses if it's necessary."

She pursed her lips. "Wow. I never knew that. I assumed all technology was forbidden."

"Like I said, it depends on the district. The bishop is allowed to decide what is right for his people."

"I hate to burden your family." What if they didn't like her? Or worse, what if they were cold to Shelby? She'd seen enough rudeness to last her a lifetime, thank you very much. She could handle it. But she couldn't accept willingly bringing Shelby somewhere she wouldn't be welcomed.

"Don't worry about it. My parents love children. They are some of the kindest people you'll ever meet."

She had nothing except his word to go on. Did she trust him enough to agree to this harebrained scheme of his? Glancing over beneath her lashes, she sighed. Maybe she was a fool, but yes, she trusted him. He'd promised her he would do his best to keep them safe, and he was risking his own life for them. He'd never intentionally hurt them.

"Fine. We'll go to your family's house."

He squeezed her hand. "My family is not like your mom. They will love Shelby. There will be no judgment."

Her jaw dropped. She snapped it closed. He'd understood her real fear. How? No one had ever understood before. Touched, she cleared her throat. "Thank you."

He removed his hand and continued driving. She curled her hands in her lap, missing the warmth his touch had brought. She turned and stared unseeingly out the window. The longer they stayed together, the rougher the inevitable separation would be. Shelby was becoming attached to him. She'd never had a father figure in her life before. Micah would make a wonderful father, but not to her daughter.

She prayed for a quick end to this case.

Micah stopped at a small convenience store. He parked the SUV between two large trucks and grabbed a dark hoodie out of his hatchback. Shoving a baseball cap on his head, he layered the hood over the cap. He was still gorgeous, just less obvious.

"Stay low," he warned her. She nodded, watching him stride into the store, keeping his head tucked inside his hood. She wished they were still in his rental car. His shiny new SUV was fancy and fun to ride in, but it stuck out a mile. They needed something inconspicuous.

She got into the back with Shelby and unhooked the seat buckle. "Come on, Sweet Pea. Let's play hide-and-seek, yes? We'll hide down here and wait for Marshal Micah to come and find us."

Shelby giggled. "Mama, this isn't a very good hiding space. He'll see us if he looks through the window."

Grimacing, she refrained from talking. They needed to remain quiet. If Micah got back without getting caught, they'd have a shot at arriving at his parents' house in one piece. Never in her life could she have imagined that her life would resemble the crime scenes she worked on.

Shelby soon became restless. Fearful someone outside would hear her, Lissa told her a story, making it up as she went along.

"Mama, horses can't do that," Shelby corrected, her voice overly loud in the quiet space.

"Shush. It's just a story. Fiction doesn't have to be real." Seeing the storm cloud on her daughter's brow, she hurried to change the scenario. That was one of the challenges of having a gifted child. Shelby remembered everything. She was easily bored and frequently fussy.

The door handle rattled. Lissa froze, fear bubbling up inside. Micah stepped into the vehicle. His voice mumbled something. She moved to where she could see him.

"I didn't hear that." She kept her voice low.

"I said don't come up here yet. I'll stop after we're out of view."

It made her nervous, not having Shelby in her car seat, but she didn't argue. They were being targeted and didn't know exactly where the next danger would come from. They'd not expected Gage, or whoever wanted to kill her, to hire a girl to kidnap her.

Once they were out of the parking lot, he pulled over and let her buckle Shelby in again before she joined him in the front seat. One look at her face told her whatever he needed to tell her was bad news.

"What happened?" She clasped her hands together in her lap to keep them from shaking.

"I got the phone my superior told me to get. The man at the counter had the TV on." He glanced back at Shelby. She was happily playing with Sonny. "The girl who'd attacked you earlier? They found her body. The cop who'd arrested her is in the hospital. It was a drive-by shooting. The news anchor suggested it was a random act of violence. We know better."

She clutched at her throat, unable to speak. It wasn't

random. It was a deliberate kill to ensure that woman couldn't identify who had hired her.

Twisting her head back and forth against the head-rest, Lissa moaned. "When will it end, Micah? Who knows how many others he's killed besides his intended calendar targets? How many will die before he gets caught?"

Or worse—what if he never got caught?

"I really don't think this was Gage. He's never been that ambitious." Even as she said it, doubt assailed her. She'd misjudged people before.

"I'm not saying you're wrong. But it's a lead we have to follow." He handed her the bag he'd brought back with him. "Can you do me a favor and set this up? I need to use it to call Marshal Hendrix tonight."

Opening the bag, she pulled out the phone. Using his pocketknife, she opened the thick plastic packaging. "They could make these easier to remove from the package."

He laughed but didn't comment.

Grabbing the directions, Lissa focused on getting the burner phone working.

"I'll never get those twenty minutes back," she told him when she finished, handing him his new phone. "Those directions were confusing and way too tiny for normal human eyes to read."

He smirked. "Maybe you need reading glasses."

"Please."

He handed her the phone back and had her dial for him. He thanked her when she handed it back and hit Call.

She tensed as she sat next to him waiting. Every nerve

in her body was on alert. It seemed every time she turned around, another danger had found them.

Stop. She couldn't continue this way. She forced herself to settle back against her seat. It was difficult, but she needed to give him space to do his job.

Still, her eyes never left his face. If his superior had bad news, or if another threat showed its face, she'd be ready.

He was tempted to put the phone on speaker, but didn't want to risk having Shelby overhear anything inappropriate for a five-year-old. The phone rang three times before it was picked up.

"Hello?"

"It's me, sir. Micah."

"Micah. Glad to hear from you. Did you hear about the woman who attacked you earlier?"

"I did. It's a shame." He could never take any death lightly. Even someone who had committed such crimes. He'd had to kill once, while he was in the army. He'd been in a situation where he needed to shoot to defend himself. The army said it was a lawful kill. But it had broken something in him to take a life. It was never easy.

"It was a shame." The sound of rustling papers carried over the line. "The records you'd requested came through."

He sat straighter, holding the phone tight. "Gage Wilson's records?"

"You got it. Let me read the important parts to you."

Marshal Hendrix's deep voice read through the record. At the age of thirteen, Gage had already been arrested for drugs and assault. Micah frowned. Gage had been a very troubled kid. He'd been in and out of juvenile hall multiple times. He was taken from his abusive father and placed in foster care at the age of ten.

Despite what he might have become as an adult, sympathy stirred for the young boy who'd been in a world with no hope.

He tamped down the sympathy. What was in the past couldn't be changed. Right now, he had a job to do and two people to protect.

"I'll call again at a later time." He glanced around. Lissa was watching Shelby, but he knew she was listening to every word he said. Tension radiated from her posture.

The marshal sighed. "It's just me, Micah. You can tell me where you're going. I need to know where to find you. I won't use your real phone. I'll use this burner phone."

He surrendered, knowing his boss was right. "I'm taking her to my family, Marshal. It's a very rural area. They won't expect her to show up there."

"That might work. Keep me posted."

He disconnected, then thought over the conversation. He was especially disturbed at another death. The body count was high.

"When will we get to your parents' house? You've taken so many back roads, I have no clue where we are."

He laughed. "I've been taking the scenic route, just in case someone is tailing us."

"Scenic route? You've turned so many times, I'm not sure even you know where we are. Some of these paths probably aren't even on any maps."

"I know exactly where we are."

He flipped on his turn signal and turned right into his parents' driveway. He saw the white house with the wraparound porch first. Past the house, a large red barn stood, a buggy at its entrance. Cows and the horse were in the pasture. A second barn lay beyond the first one. It was smaller than the first, and it served as his *daed*'s carpentry shop. He'd spent many hours in that shop as a boy and teenager. His parents had planned for him to take his place with his father. That hadn't happened. He'd thought he'd come to terms with his sister's disappearance. But when he was a teenager, another child had vanished. He hadn't known the child well, but the mother had once been a friend of their family. Micah had experienced a resurgence of nightmares. They plagued him nightly. Some kids had found the younger child's body, and Micah hadn't been able to stop wondering if his sister Christina had suffered a similar fate.

He'd blamed himself. Staying in that house, seeing his mother's face, and believing he was the reason her baby girl was missing, he'd left rather than stare at her agony for the rest of his life.

He knew, logically, that he hadn't been to blame. He'd been a mere child himself. But sometimes emotions weren't logical.

Enough. He was where God had put him. If he had remained Amish, he wouldn't be able to help Lissa now. His parents' home was an option only because he was with the US Marshals.

His *mamm* came out on the porch, wiping her hands on a faded dish towel. She was still lovely, after all these years. Her dark hair was streaked with gray under her crisp white prayer *kapp*. The crow's feet fanning out around her eyes grew more pronounced each year. But she still had a beautiful warm smile, the same smile she'd passed on to Joss, her daughter.

"Micah," she called. "I didn't know you'd be here. Its *gut* to see you, my *sohn*. Your father and Gideon are in the shop."

"I hope it's not a bother that I showed up unannounced." He paused outside Lissa's door.

"*Ack*. No, it's *gut*. I always enjoy seeing you. It's no trouble." While she talked, Edith Bender leaned to the right, trying to get a look at the passengers inside his car. "Who do you have with you, Micah? Did you bring your sister for a visit?"

He opened the door and helped Lissa out. Then he moved to the back. Shelby had unbuckled her seat and burst out of the car the moment the door opened. Edith's eyes twinkled, although he could see questions in their depths.

"No, *Mamm*. I didn't bring Joss. This is my friend Lissa and her little girl, Shelby. Shelby, can you say hi to my *mamm*?"

She tilted her head and considered Edith. "Ma'am?"

Lissa chuckled. "She's thinking *ma'am* like *sir* or *ma'am*." Micah laughed. "Shelby, this is Marshal Micah's mama. But she's Amish, so he says *Mamm*, not Mama."

She pursed her lips. "Why is she Amish? Marshal Micah's not Amish."

Beside him, Lissa groaned softly. He bit his lips to hide a smile. A quick glance confirmed that her cheeks were flushed.

He turned his attention to the little girl and answered her question. "I'm not Amish anymore, Shelby. I used to be when I was your age."

Shelby seemed to accept this and stopped asking questions. She apparently decided she and Edith were destined to be friends, though, because she marched up to the older woman and held out her beloved pony. "This is my pony, Sonny. Want to hold him?"

Edith laughed gently, "Sweet child, I would love to hold your pony. *Cumme*, all of you. Micah, you can explain after we eat, ain't so?"

"Yes, *Mamm*."

She'd always assumed that dinner in an Amish house would be a somber meal. A meal at the Bender table was anything but. Micah's brother Gideon overflowed with high spirits and mischievousness. She laughed so hard at his stories, she had tears running down her cheeks at one point and her stomach muscles began to ache.

Micah surprised her, as well. He fit in with his family as if he'd never left. He gave Gideon as much grief as his younger brother dished out and treated his parents with affection and respect.

The first time Nathan Bender, Micah's father, had tuned his bright blue eyes, so like his son's, on her, Lissa had been sure she'd find judgment or distaste. Not that they knew her past, but after her own mother had tossed her out, she'd become overly sensitive. Sometimes, it felt like she was wearing a sign that said she was unworthy. So even though she knew it was ridiculous, part of her waited to be slapped down again. It never happened. Nathan welcomed her and Shelby as if they were hon-

ore

Stopphonacr

---

ored to have them sitting at the table. She'd never experienced this level of graciousness before.

Micah waited until Lissa had returned from putting Shelby to bed before he began explaining to his parents what brought them to their house. Lissa fought back the tears as he mentioned Tracy. His parents gasped when he told them about the Birthday Card Killer. Listening to him speak, such a wild story seemed too incredible to believe. And yet it was all true.

Again, she waited for the negative reaction. After all, a murderer had her in his sights. Any danger to her could and would affect their family while she was among them. Edith stood and approached her, then the older woman placed her arms around Lissa and rocked her close as if she were no more than a child.

It had been a long time since Lissa had experienced a mother's hug. The emotion rocketing around inside her leaked out her eyes.

It wasn't until she was in bed that night that Lissa realized Micah hadn't told her about Gage's juvenile record. She had caught enough of his conversation with the Marshal to know it had been released to him.

He hadn't seemed satisfied with it. Which meant there was nothing in the records that proved a murderous pattern or proved Gage was or wasn't a cold-blooded killer.

THIRTEEN

It was at breakfast the next morning when Lissa met Micah's other brother Zeke and his wife, Iris. Zeke struck her as a kindhearted man, but very quiet. Where Gideon laughed and chattered, Zeke smiled and considered what was said before he spoke. His opinions were thoughtful and concise. Lissa couldn't help but like him. He was the ideal older brother.

Meeting Iris, however, was a totally different story. Iris wasn't just quiet. There was something cold in her manner. She didn't encourage sharing. Lissa wanted out of her company within minutes of meeting the other woman.

Not that Iris was mean. She wasn't. She was abstract and aloof, but not unkind. She made Lissa uncomfortable.

"Today we should bake some pies. Would you like that, Lissa?" Edith asked.

Interest sparked. "Yes, I would, actually. I've always enjoyed baking."

She didn't elaborate upon her goal to open a restaurant. Maybe had Edith been alone she would have. But with Iris listening over her shoulder, the less said the better.

They gathered all the supplies they needed in the kitchen and got to work. Soon the aromas of their efforts filled the air. They had finished the crusts and were working on the lattice work for the top of the pie when Edith realized she had run out of her favorite pie spice. "Iris, can you go to the store at the Zooks' and get some?"

When Iris moved to gather her cloak from a peg near the door, Edith turned to Lissa. "The store is down the road half a mile. Why don't you join her?"

Lissa's first thought was to refuse. "Oh, but Shelby—"

"She'll be fine here with me. You girls will be gone for thirty minutes. Maybe forty. It's that close. Have you ever seen an Amish store before?"

She hadn't. She had to admit, it was tempting. And with the store so close, it probably wouldn't hurt. She bit her lip, unable to decide what to do.

"I'm leaving now." Iris's voice was quiet. The floor vibrated with the force of the door closing. Gathering her courage, Lissa gathered an old cloak of Edith's and headed out the door. She ran to catch up with Iris. They didn't talk the few minutes it took to walk to the store. Lissa was too busy categorizing all the colors and smells in her mind to care if Iris liked her or not.

For the first time in days, the sun was out and shining so bright that she had to squint as she followed Iris to the store. The air was cool still, but Lissa imagined the vitamin D hitting her skin in waves. Her mood lifted. She swung her arms while she walked, grateful to be alive to enjoy this beautiful day.

When they entered the store, the woman behind the counter glanced up and greeted Iris by name before aiming a friendly smile Lissa's way. Iris returned the greeting politely but didn't stop to chat. By the way the woman had immediately returned to her book, this was normal behavior. Iris lifted a shopping basket from beside the door and then walked directly to an aisle at the other side of the store. She found the items Edith wanted with the unerring efficiency born of familiarity.

Lissa wanted to ask her to slow down and give her a chance to browse the small store with its hand-packaged items. The woman who'd dreamed of one day becoming a chef was thrilled at the selection of baking items. However, it was obvious that Iris desired to be finished with their little shopping excursion. Lissa didn't want to be a bother. Nor did she want to bring any more attention to herself. She kept her wish to herself and followed Iris to the cash register.

The woman behind the counter murmured to Iris. Lissa had trouble hearing her voice. That was when she realized she hadn't heard much since they'd left the house.

Her batteries had gotten too low. Last night, she'd connected the battery charger Micah had picked up for her, but they hadn't taken the battery pack to the carpentry shop to fully charge it. Since she never used a battery charger for her cochlear implants, it hadn't occurred to her that she needed to do it. She'd hooked up her charger to the battery pack, seen the red lights indicating it was working, and had fallen into bed and slept clear through until morning.

When she'd woken, she'd grabbed them and put them on by feel. She should have looked to see what level the indicator lights were at. Now it was too late. She couldn't hear a thing.

Glancing at Iris, she saw the woman's mouth move as she talked to the other woman. Maybe Iris hadn't been as silent as she'd thought, Lissa realized. Maybe she'd tried talking and Lissa hadn't heard her. She'd have to apologize once they were outside. She didn't want to offend Micah's sister-in-law.

When Iris picked up her plastic shopping bag and turned to exit the store, she flashed a confused look at Lissa. Now she was sure of it. The other woman had tried talking to her. They departed. Lissa held out a hand, halting the other woman. Iris looked at her cautiously. Lissa felt horrid. She was probably feeling self-conscious after being ignored, from her point of view.

"I'm sorry if you said anything and I didn't respond," Lissa began. It was odd knowing you were talking, but not hearing a sound. Only muscle memory helped her know she wasn't yelling at the other woman. She took a deep breath, trying to stave off the panic brewing below the surface. She used her hands to uncover the processors magnetically attached to both sides of her head. "I'm profoundly deaf and wear cochlear implants, and last night, they didn't charge. I can't hear anything right now. I'm sorry."

Iris's rigid facial muscles relaxed, melting into a warmer smile. "Can you read lips?"

She spoke with exaggerated slowness.

"Yes, some. Please speak at a normal pace."

The other woman nodded. "I understand. I was afraid I'd made you angry. You weren't answering any of my questions. I know I'm shy and don't talk much, not like my husband's family."

Lissa's worry dissolved. "I'm definitely not mad. Just anxious to get home and charge my processors. Micah took the charger to the shop to charge it this morning."

The other woman smiled her understanding, and they began to walk. They didn't talk much. It was hard holding a conversation and read lips while walking, especially on uneven terrain. The road was rough with dips and potholes. She could see herself tripping and embarrassing herself even more. She didn't have an endless supply of clothes with her. She would need to wash the clothes she and her daughter had worn the day before. Dismayed, she realized she wouldn't be able to stick them in the dryer. She'd have to hang them out to dry. Glancing again at the blue, sunny sky, she crossed her fingers that the weather would stay dry.

They were halfway between the store and the Bender house when she stopped, cold sweat breaking out on her forehead.

Iris saw her and also halted.

"Lissa?" she saw her mouth.

Lissa grabbed the other woman's arm and pulled her away from the road. It was all she could do not to run, but she didn't want to draw any more attention to herself. Thankfully, Iris didn't argue. Together, they speed-walked to a clump of trees.

Lissa hunkered down into a squat, making herself as small as she possibly could. Her calves protested, but she ignored them. This was literally life-and-death.

Iris tapped her shoulder. She turned her gaze to the other woman, who seemed impossibly young all of a sudden. Iris held both hands, palm up, out at her shoulders in a universal gesture for "What's going on?"

Lissa whispered, hoping her voice wasn't carrying. "Do you see that person on the motorcycle talking to a teenager on the street?"

Iris followed her gaze. She blanched. "That boy is my brother."

Lissa wanted to scream. She leaned her head against the tree trunk for just a moment, trying to catch her breath.

Iris caught her arm. "Who is that? Is that the person trying to kill you?"

"I don't know. I can't see his face. I've never seen his face. The last time I saw him he was on an ATV." If she'd had even one working cochlear implant this morning, she would have heard the motorcycle.

Terror filled Iris's face. Her body trembled next to Lissa's. She was like a deer sensing danger, ready to take flight.

Lissa recalled her cell phone in her pocket.

She could send Micah a text. Scrambling to get it from her pocket, she unlocked it and immediately put it on silent mode. All she needed was for someone to try and call her, giving away their location. Then she punched out a simple text to Micah, praying he'd get it and be able to act fast. Normally, she typed with care, because she tended to make a lot of typos when she didn't pay attention. She didn't have time to be careful. She had to get away and she desperately wanted to ensure that Iris's brother was out of danger.

There was nothing more she could do.

Micah held the end of the two-by-four for his *daed* while the older man sawed it. His grip tightened the moment before the saw bit through the final length of the plywood, prepared for the expected kickback.

His *daed* picked the piece of wood up, examining it for any flaws, before he smiled widely at Micah.

The shop door swung open, letting the cool air and Zeke into the dusty work area.

"Zeke! *Welkum, sohn.*" The older man held his board aloft. "Your brother and I are having trouble with this, *ja*? We've cut it twice, and when I measure it, it's still too short."

Zeke and Micah both shook their heads. Their *daed* had been cracking that same joke their entire lives.

"Did you stop by the house?" Micah set the board in his hands to the side.

"Ja. I did. *Mamm* and the women are baking pies. It smells wonderful *gut* in there. I also stopped and checked on the foal. He's a strong, healthy one, ain't so? Will you sell him, *daed*?"

Zeke hadn't gone into the carpentry business with his father and younger brother. He trained under the local farrier, working on horse hooves and shoeing them, keeping their feet healthy. An important job, when the Amish community relied heavily on their horses, both on the farms and to haul the buggies anytime they traveled.

"I might keep this one. For now. He's a *gut* horse. The mare is getting old. She'll need to be replaced in a few years."

His phone vibrated in his pocket. Not his burner phone. The real one. Curious to see who'd be texting him, he took the device out and unlocked it. The blood rushed from his head when he read the message.

"Micah!" His father's voice sounded like it was coming through a long tunnel. "Micah, what is it, *sohn*?"

He held out his phone. "Lissa and Iris walked to the store. They are hiding in the trees right now because someone on a motorcycle stopped to talk with Iris's brother, Danny. Lissa thinks it might be the man after her."

Zeke was already running for the door. Micah hurried after him. Catching his brother, he slowed him down. "What are you going to do, Zeke? If it is him, and you go charging over there, you could get Danny and the women shot. Think, man! We need to be careful. Their lives depend on it."

He could see the fight instinct struggling with his upbringing. Zeke's shoulders slumped. Micah ran to his SUV, glad he'd had the foresight to move it inside the garage last night. He grabbed his second gun from the glove box and shoved it in the back of his waistband. He dashed back to where Zeke stood. To his surprise, his brother didn't say anything about the extra gun he'd pulled from the vehicle.

"Go into the house," he told his brother. "Tell *Mamm* to keep Shelby in the house. I will be back soon."

He didn't wait to watch and see if his brother complied. Zeke had a cool head. He'd do what he was asked. That left Micah to go and save the two women and Danny. Keeping to the trees along the side of the road, he edged his way toward the store, keeping low so the man wouldn't see him coming.

Soon, he heard Danny's voice. "I haven't seen anyone like that." Danny's voice was friendly and helpful. The kid didn't realize he was in grave danger.

"Are you sure? I'm sure my sister said her boyfriend lives on this street."

He was trying to find Lissa. He was sure of it. The man knew enough to know Micah had lived here. Which meant he knew Micah had been Amish.

A large truck honked. The motorcycle's engine revved, then sped off in the other direction. Micah growled. He'd been so close to him, but he couldn't risk firing a gun on this road. There were kids outside playing in the yards. A woman across the road was hanging up laundry.

But where were Lissa and Iris?

He stepped out of his cover and ran over to Danny. The boy was a tall, reed-thin fourteen-year-old. "Hey, Danny."

"Micah." Awareness lit his eyes. "Oh! I think that man was searching for you. When he said his sister was dating a police officer, it never occurred to me he meant you. You're not police, *ja*?"

"I'm not. Danny, that man is dangerous. If you see him again, don't talk to him or tell him any information. He needs to be in jail."

Whatever Danny might have said was silenced when his sister cried out his name. Danny and Micah glanced down the street and watched Iris and Lissa racing toward them. Iris flung her arms around her brother, scolding him and kissing his cheek simultaneously. Flushing, the boy squirmed, trying to escape his sister.

Lissa hurled herself at Micah. When she grabbed him around the waist and burrowed her face into his shirt, he instinctively wrapped his arms around her and held tight. She was shaking so hard, it was a wonder she could stand.

"Lissa?" No response. That worried him.

"She can't hear you." Iris's voice was thick, fuzzy with unshed tears. "She told me her cochlear implants were both dead."

"Ah."

Putting his finger under her chin, he gently raised her face. It was white, but surprisingly, no tears trailed down her cheeks. Probably too scared to cry.

"Lissa, Shelby's in the house with my mom. Let's go inside. You can tell me what happened, and then I'll call my boss, Marshal Hendrix, and see if we can't get some law out here to search. We're close."

She nodded. But didn't move. He stared at her for ten seconds before giving in and bending over, gently kissing her.

It was the shortest kiss in history, broken up by a smart-aleck teenage boy making gagging sounds.

"Enough." Micah laughed, tucked Lissa's cold hand in his, then headed back to his parents' house. "We have to move quickly."

A sense of urgency skittered across his nerves. They were standing out in the open and he still didn't know what had scared Lissa and Iris. Gripping her hand tighter, he tugged her faster. They were vulnerable and needed to get inside before they became the pawns in a deadly game of target practice.

FOURTEEN

There wasn't anything more to be said until they arrived in the house. Lissa ran inside to check on Shelby. She returned to the kitchen with her implant processors and her charger in her hand. "You said you have electricity in the shop, right? I need this plugged in. Even if it charges for a couple of hours that should give me enough juice to last."

He couldn't imagine what she must be feeling, to be sitting here, knowing a killer was nearby, and having her hearing stripped away. He took the bundle from her and hurried to the shop. Wiping the thin coat of dust off the counter area near the electrical outlets, he plugged in her device, then returned to the house.

The rich scent of coffee permeated the air. His mother had made breakfast, but he could see most of the adults in the room had no desire for food at the moment. "We should eat." He kept his face toward Lissa, although he meant his comments for everyone. "This could be a long day."

Lissa stretched out her hand and grabbed a biscuit. She buttered it and broke off a small piece with her fingers. When she popped it into her mouth, her eyes widened. His mother made the best biscuits he'd ever had. He helped himself to some more coffee, then settled in to hear Lissa and Iris. They took turns explaining the events of the past hour.

Micah stood and went into the other room to call his boss.

"You're late," Hendrix said when he picked up the phone. "I expected your call twenty minutes ago."

"Sorry, sir. It couldn't be helped." Succinctly, he described the morning's adventure. Hendrix listened, interrupting only twice for clarification. "Hold tight, Micah. Don't go outside. Keep everyone away from the windows. I'm sending reinforcements."

"I'll do my best, sir. But if the killer is asking about us, it's only a matter of time before someone remembers that I'm a deputy marshal and asks him if that's what he means."

"Well, for now, it appears our suspect is unaware of your exact title, which helps us as it adds to the confusion. We're on it."

Micah returned to the room and told them what the top marshal in the district had said.

Within thirty minutes, Parker banged on the back door. Micah went to answer, bringing his partner into the kitchen and introducing him to the rest of the family.

"So, what's happening out there?" Micah asked.

Parker raised his eyebrows, deliberately glancing around the table full of his family, silently asking if he really wanted to have that conversation in present company. Micah waved his concerns away.

"This is my family, Parker, and they are rightly concerned. This affects them, and their safety. They need to know."

He wouldn't budge on that. He was risking a lot, staying with his parents. In his defense, he hadn't thought his background, growing up in an Amish community, was well-known. It wasn't as if he talked about his family a great deal. He liked to keep his personal life private.

He'd made an error there. He wasn't about to make another one and keep them out of the loop. The Amish didn't fight. His father wouldn't use violence to defend himself or his family. But he would hide if he needed to. Nathan Bender was clever. And he was observant. If someone was seen nosing around the property, he'd know to make sure he and his family were not available to be questioned.

Parker puffed his cheeks and blew out a breath, hard. Clearly, he didn't agree with Micah's assessment. But he also wouldn't argue.

"Okay, so your friend on the motorcycle," he began, and Micah scoffed at the word *friend*. Parker continued, "...has been seen around here asking questions. But he seems to have gone. We can't find him, nor does anyone agree on which direction he was headed. No description since he never removed his helmet. Seems strange, I know, but he clearly didn't want to be identified. We're still searching. Unfortunately, I don't know where you should go."

"Go?" Lissa asked. "Are we leaving again?"

"We can't stay here." Micah turned to her so she could read his lips. "I don't know which direction he's gone in, though. We stick out, and if he sees us in my car…"

"Then leave your car here," Edith said. "You still have Amish clothes. I can find something that will fit Lissa and Shelby. He won't be looking for an Amish couple with *kind*, ain't so?"

Could it be that simple? Could they really disguise themselves in plain sight?

"I still don't think we should stay here. He knew that I had grown up on this road." Only the fact that Danny hadn't known they were here and that he'd been looking for a cop had kept him away from the family farm.

"*Cumme* to my *haus*."

Micah stared at his brother. "Zeke? Are you sure?"

"*Ja.* I live close by, but not so close that he'd think to look there. And the people in our community are not going to give out information about you to some *Englisch* stranger asking a lot of questions."

He cleared his throat, moved by his brother's words. "But I'm not Amish. Not anymore."

"*Ack.*" Edith narrowed her eyes. "You don't live here, *ja*, that's true. But you are still my *sohn*, *ja*? Our neighbors know you. They know us. They don't know this person nosing into your business."

When Edith Bender spoke with her eyes narrowed like that, no one in the family argued with her. Not even Nathan.

She scoured the upstairs bedrooms for clothes for Lissa. She was close to the same size as Edith, so she found something. Then she showed her how to fix her hair under the *kapp*. Micah's jaw dropped open when he saw the transformation.

Iris ran across the street and borrowed a dress and a *kapp* from her cousin Stella. They were perfect for Shelby. It took nearly fifteen minutes to convince Shelby to wear the clothes, however. She liked to climb trees, she told them, and girls couldn't climb trees in a dress.

Micah knew he shouldn't smile at her antics. She was the most adorable child he'd ever met, though, even if she was stubborn. She probably got that from Lissa.

Speaking of Lissa, she was still deaf. He left the house, now dressed as an Amish man, and headed to his father's shop. His muscles bunched. He fought the urge to hurry. That was not the Amish way. His shoulders flinched. He could almost imagine a target on his back. He sighed and flexed his shoulder muscles once inside the second barn.

Grabbing the device and charger, he hoped it had charged long enough for Lissa to hear. He should have charged the battery pack when they'd arrived, but they'd been tired and overwhelmed by all that had happened in such a brief time.

Micah halted, his eyes fastened on the calendar on the wall. It was May 1.

Lissa's birthday month. He shuddered. The Birthday Card Killer was out there, looking for her, determined to end her life. Micah bent his head, silently praying for protection.

And for this villain to be brought to justice before any more blood was shed.

Lissa's heart thundered inside her chest. She'd pulled out her phone, checking to see if Micah had texted her. He'd been gone longer than she'd expected.

That was when she saw the date. She felt a meta-phorical noose tighten around her throat. He was out there, looking for her. How many people would get hurt while she was on his radar?

The thought that it might be, that it probably was, someone she knew curdled her stomach. How did you work with someone, talk and laugh with someone, and not know that they were capable of that kind of evil?

For she was now convinced she knew the killer. In her mind, just out of reach, she sensed a hint of a mem-ory of Tracy's crime scene. She could envision herself standing in the kitchen. She could see the mess on the floor, the blood and the dust used to capture prints, the crime scene tape fluttering in the window.

She could even remember the feeling of someone standing behind her. What she couldn't remember was if she turned to face the person before they'd attacked. What had she seen?

Did it matter? Micah seemed to believe she'd been picked as the next victim even before Tracy had been murdered.

The vibrations on the floor warned her someone was treading her way. A second later Micah appeared in the doorway. A flush warmed her cheeks. They'd never talked about the very brief kiss they'd shared outside. What had she been thinking?

Apparently, nothing. Or it never would have hap-pened. The look in his eyes told her his mind had gone in the same direction, remembering the feeling of their lips touching.

He shook himself, then held out his hand.

"My processors." She grabbed them and quickly removed the white *kapp* and looped the earpiece over her ears before placing the circular magnetic component on. When she heard the soft tones telling her the device was working, she grinned. "I can hear again. What a relief!"

"Good. We should get going. My boss and Parker both know where we're going."

She still wasn't sure it was a good idea to remove to his brother's house. She didn't have much of a choice, though.

Shelby ran into the room, beaming. "Mama! I look like Micah's mama!"

Chucking, she bent and kissed the grinning child. "You do. I think you look lovely."

Even dressed Amish, the little toy pony was clutched tightly in her grip. One of these days, that horse was going to be so well loved she'd need to sew him back together. She could see that one of his ears was beginning to unravel.

Kind of reminded her of her life.

Micah helped her and Shelby pile into the buggy. The blue leather seats were unexpected. She'd imagined they'd be sitting on hard benches. While they were not the most comfortable seats, these padded benches reminded her of sitting on the chairs in the old church social hall.

The jolt of the buggy's movement was hard to get used to. She used her arms to brace herself as she swayed with the carriage. It was only a ten-minute drive, but she still felt like she'd been on the water when Micah helped down from the buggy. Any longer, she might have gotten seasick. She chuckled silently. She'd been under so much stress, she was getting silly. When this was over, she and Shelby would need a holiday.

Micah ushered them inside the house the moment Shelby bounced down from the buggy. She at least had loved the ride. She wanted to ride the horses, she told Zeke.

"Sorry, little one," he smiled at her, his blue eyes crinkling at the corner. "We don't ride our horses. That mare is for pulling our buggy, and that's it."

Disappointed, the child sighed. "She's such a pretty horse."

Lissa agreed with her daughter. The dappled mare was stunning. Her coloring reminded Lissa of a newborn fawn, or a sunlit meadow.

"Come on, Sweet Pea. Marshal Micah says we need to go in the house."

Shelby went without arguing, amazing her mother. When the child skipped ahead and caught Micah's hand, her heart caught in her chest. Lissa rubbed her chest, trying to smooth the ache away. The adoring glance Shelby gave the tall lawman made her throat feel swollen with emotion. She bit her lip, forcing herself to be calm.

Inside, though, worry nestled deep in her soul. Soon, very soon, this would all end, and hopefully, the killer would spend the rest of his life in a very tiny jail cell. When that happened, her daughter would be bereft. Because Micah would disappear from their lives.

Lissa wouldn't even see him at work. She had made her decision. She could never go back to being a crime scene cleaner. Never again would she walk into the place where someone had died and calmly erase the evidence of what had happened.

She had no clue as to what she'd do. But she knew in the deepest corner of her soul God wanted her to move on.

Hours later, Parker showed up on the front porch. He pulled Micah and Lissa outside to talk. Her pulse kicked up. Would he tell her all was well?

"He got away."

Her heart sank.

"We've searched and he's nowhere in sight. I think tomorrow the boss plans to move Shelby and Lissa into full protective custody."

Micah blanched.

"Micah, what does that mean?"

"It means you'll be put into a safe house, possibly given new identities, until it's safe to return."

"Will you go with us?"

He shook his head. "I will stay here."

Her heart dropped like lead. She knew that look on his face. "You haven't failed us."

She started to say more. Her words were cut short, however, when an arrow whizzed past her and buried itself into the column next to her head.

"Get down!" Micah yelled. He grabbed her hand and pulled her off the porch, behind the buggy sitting in the driveway.

Lissa squatted down beside the black buggy so fast, she nearly scraped her cheek on the matte-finished surface. A second arrow sailed through the air. The arrow struck the other side of the buggy but didn't pierce it.

Parker stood and fired a shot. Micah ran to the front of the buggy and fired his gun toward the trees. For a few minutes, there was silence. Then they heard the motorcycle. It headed in the opposite direction.

"We need to move you now."

Micah's face was colder than she'd ever seen it. The man she'd grown to care for had sealed himself off.

The next hour, all she could do was wait. Micah was constantly on the phone. Trying to hammer out the details of where they would go next. She couldn't get a full breath. Her life was at a crossroads, and she faced either death or going into hiding, separated from the man she lo—

She wouldn't go there.

Micah was getting ready to send her off with his replacement when someone knocked on the door. A marshal she'd never seen before entered the room.

"Marshal Hendrix." Both Parker and Micah rose.

"Men. Miss Page. It's over."

Her mouth dropped. "What?"

"Gage Wilson's body was discovered an hour ago. His house was searched. He had committed suicide. Evidence was found in the form of pictures and notes he'd written. He was our man."

She could barely process what he was saying.

"I can go home?" she choked out.

"Yes, Miss Page. We can close this case and you can go home and move on with your life."

She didn't hear anything more.

Gage Wilson was dead. It was done. Lissa and Shelby could return to their life. But what would Micah do?

Would he walk out of their lives after the paperwork was done? Would she see him again or would this be her last memory of him?

FIFTEEN

"I'm done." Micah wiped his mouth on a cloth napkin and pushed his plate away. Out of the corner of his eye, he saw Lissa hunch in an attempt to stifle a snicker. He grinned at her, knowing what she was thinking. Old habits were hard to break. "It was delicious, Mamm."

"Especially the cinnamon rolls." Gideon laughed. "You ate two of them."

Micah shrugged. It was true. "Well, I couldn't let them go to waste, now, could I?"

Shelby giggled into her hands. She sat between Micah and her mother. Grinning, he winked at the child. Lissa rolled her eyes.

His mother beamed. "It is *gut* to have you here at our table, Micah. You can eat anything you want. There's more bacon."

Content, he patted his flat stomach. "Thank you, *Mamm*. I'm stuffed."

"Marshal Micah, you can have the rest of my cinnamon roll, if you want it. My tummy's full."

He caught his breath at the sweetness of her. He reached over and rubbed her head under the *kapp*. After today, she could take the Amish clothes off without fear. Regret warred with satisfaction at a job well done. He'd kept his promise and protected them from harm.

He might not have a place in their lives, but at least he had that. When he raised his gaze and met Lissa's, he was surprised to see her brow furrowed. When he mouthed, "What's wrong?"

She pointed to her ear and shook her head.

"It's fine," he mouthed. She nodded.

He could have a place in their lives, if he could convince Lissa to let him in. He knew she loved him. Didn't she? She'd never said it, but the soft smile she shared with him told him she wasn't immune to him. Shivers of longing coursed through him. If only he could share simple times like this with them every day. If he had the right of a husband and father, he wouldn't have to leave them. Ever.

"Micah," his father interrupted his musings. "Before you leave, I'd like your help in the shop. Between Gideon, you and I, it wouldn't take more than an hour or so. That's not too much time, ain't?"

"Of course, I can help. It's not even eight thirty. Even if it takes a couple of hours, we can make it back to Lissa's place by noon."

Lissa broke into the conversation. "I called my boss this morning. I'm not scheduled to work again until tomorrow, so regardless of what time you finish, we'll still be good."

Nathan grinned, his mouth stretching wide enough to crinkle the corners of his eyes. "That's *gut*."

The adults rose from the table. Lissa instructed Shelby to leave Sonny on the bench and help Edith clear the table. He smiled to himself. It felt like a home. His *daed* was waiting for him. First, though, he needed to check on Lissa. He motioned for her to follow him.

When she joined him in the hall, he held back a smile. She was adorable, dressed in her Amish dress and *kapp*.

"Were you able to charge your implants last night?"

She nodded. "Yep. They're both working perfectly. It was a little noisy at the table, and Shelby's voice is soft, so I wasn't sure what she'd said. But her expression was serious, so I was worried something was wrong."

"Nothing wrong. She offered me part of her cinnamon roll. Apparently, she was concerned that I would waste away from hunger."

She chuckled. "That's good. She's so funny. I love that she was willing to share. Your mother's cinnamon rolls are the best I've ever tasted."

He couldn't deny that.

Standing so close to her, he couldn't think of anything else to say. She had a speck of maple icing on her full lower lip. He should back up and go help his father.

He didn't. Instead, he stared into her eyes. When her breathing hitched, he stopped fighting and bent his head and brushed his mouth against hers. It was a featherlight caress. Her lips were as sweet as he'd remembered. Lifting his head, he searched her face. She smiled.

Leaning in, he captured her lips again. Her hands latched on to his biceps. He slid his arms around her waist but didn't pull her any closer. The kiss was innocent. Chaste.

It shattered him. If he'd had any doubt that she owned his heart, it crumbled to dust.

A throat cleared behind him.

As he jumped away from her, her gaze flicked behind his shoulder. A deep flush flooded her face. Spinning around, she darted into the kitchen.

"Mama, why is your face red?" Shelby's high voice carried to where he stood.

Gideon chuckled behind him. "I wondered what was taking you so long."

"I don't want to talk about it," Micah growled, stomping through the kitchen to the door. At the last minute, his eyes found Lissa's again. Her color still high, she smiled and ducked her head.

He grinned. It was a beautiful day.

Edith sat in on the couch and patted the cushion next to her. Shelby bounced over to the gentle woman and sat down beside her. When Edith grabbed a book and started to read it to the child, Lissa smiled. This was what it might have been like if Shelby had a grandmother.

The smile vanished. She shouldn't have kissed him back.

Feeling like a caged tiger, Lissa prowled around the room, looking out the windows. Shelby's grandparents, both maternal and paternal, hadn't wanted anything to do with her. They'd kicked Lissa out of their lives before Shelby had even been born.

Letting her daughter grow attached wasn't smart. The sooner they left the better off she'd be.

The better off they'd both be. Why had she kissed him?

She'd been caught by the tenderness in his gaze like a deer fixed in the beam of headlights. At that moment, she knew his feelings for her went deep. For an instant, hope had leaped alive in her heart. Before she could regain her balance, his lips had touched hers and every resolution she'd made to stay strong and emotionally distant had flown out the window.

If Gideon hadn't interrupted them, who knows how long they'd have stayed like that. Most likely, she would have stayed right where she was, kissing him and letting him farther under her skin.

Hadn't she learned her lesson with Teddy? She'd had her heart broken twice. She wasn't eager to have it broken a third time.

Micah's not like that. She hunched her shoulders, fighting back the tiny voice inside that begged her to trust him. She had Shelby to consider. It would be hard enough to explain to her daughter why Marshal Micah wasn't coming around anymore. If he stayed in her life any longer, it would be that much worse. She had to protect her daughter from that kind of heartache and disappointment.

Edith stood up from the couch. "I think someone is here."

Lissa glanced out the window. She hadn't heard anyone arrive. Craning her neck, she saw a buggy. Zeke hopped down and helped his wife down. They spoke together for a moment, and then Zeke strode away.

Less than a minute later, Edith greeted Iris as she walked in the kitchen door.

"I saw Zeke with you." Lissa said.

"Ja." Iris said, casting her gaze down. She sure was shy. "He wanted to help his *daed* and brothers."

"Nathan will be happy to have his help." Edith commented.

"Lissa." Iris said. Lissa startled. She hadn't expected Iris to address her directly. She smiled at Micah's sister-in-law and focused her attention on her face. Although her implants were functioning perfectly, Iris possessed such a soft voice that it was sometimes challenging to hear and understand everything she said without seeing her lips and expressions. "I was planning on doing some baking today. We didn't have time to get to know each other when you came to our *haus*. While the men are busy, would you like to *cumme* home with me and help?"

She didn't respond at first. She wasn't anxious to leave the house. Although she appreciated the invitation, she felt more secure in the house with Edith. Plus, Micah expected her to wait with his mother. She said as much.

"Micah will be gone for another hour," Edith said, giving her an encouraging smile. "Now that Zeke is there, he'll enjoy time with his *daed* and brothers. I'll keep your *dochter* with me, *ja*? It's been so long since I've had a little girl in the *haus*."

Joss had been abducted when she was two years old. Edith had never had the pleasure of seeing her as a five-year-old. Suddenly, turning Iris down felt selfish. How could she deny Micah a chance to bond with his brothers and Edith the joy of Shelby? Gage was dead. The danger was gone.

"Sure. I'll come."

She kissed her daughter. "Remember. You need to mind Mrs. Bender. And say please and thank you."

"I will, Mama."

Her daughter was bouncing, excited to help Micah's mother. With one last kiss, she left the house and followed Iris to their buggy. "Don't worry. You've been to our *haus*. You know we're only minutes away." Iris flicked the reins, clicking her tongue. The horse began a slow trot out of the driveway. The buggy jolted.

It was an awkward ten-minute drive. Despite inviting her, Iris wasn't inclined to talk. She remembered how silent Micah had been in the car the first time they rode together. Maybe it was an Amish habit. She settled in to enjoy the ride, but all she wanted was to turn around and return to the Bender house.

They arrived at Zeke and Iris's home, and Lissa expected Iris's attitude to warm up once they were inside. Iris made no move to gather baking supplies. Instead, she paced in front of the window, her expression pensive.

"Um, Iris? Did you want to start baking? I need to be back with my daughter in an hour."

This was a bad idea. Why had Iris invited her if she didn't plan on talking to her? As the other woman continued to pace, the uneasiness sloshing around inside Lissa strengthened into a heavy apprehension.

"I didn't want to do this." Iris finally turned and aimed a level stare at her. The shy act was gone. Her direct gaze made Lissa uneasy.

"Do what? I have no idea what you're talking about. You said you wanted help with your baking." Lissa barely knew what she was saying. She was desperate to get out of Iris's company and race to her daughter's side.

"I needed an excuse to get you here. He said it didn't matter what excuse I used."

Ice invaded her soul, stealing her breath. Something was wrong. "He? Who do you mean?"

"Good morning, Lissa."

Gasping, Lissa whirled around to find Evan standing behind her. He sneered at her. Lissa's gaze dropped briefly to his lapel, where a flashy silver pin winked at her. The memory of the crime scene rushed through her. Tracy's blood on the floor. Gage helping her and then leaving. Seeing that lapel pin on the floor, then turning to find Evan behind her, a feral snarl on his face before he lashed out and struck her with the vase.

"You killed Tracy!" she gaped at him, unwilling to believe what was clearly the truth. "Gage—"

"Gage was a useful scapegoat. I knew sooner or later you'd remember. The fact that you have a May birthday was convenient."

"My brother," Iris burst out. "You said you'd free my brother if I did this."

Evan speared the Amish woman with his cold gaze. "Your brother is safe at home. I never had him."

Iris's hands flew to her mouth. "You said you'd kill him if I didn't help you."

"I would have. Now, I won't have to." He reached into his back pocket. "You, however, won't be alive to tell anyone."

His hand flashed out, and the gun in his hand barked once.

Iris dropped to the ground. Lissa started toward her, but found her wrists grabbed in an iron grip. Evan dragged her out the door.

SIXTEEN

Lissa struggled to pull her wrists out of Evan's iron grasp. The more she yanked, the tighter he held on, until his clasp became painful. Her smartwatch dug into her wrist's tender skin.

"Let me go!" she shrieked. "She's going to die. She needs help!"

"You're right, she will." Evan glared at her. "You won't be alive much longer either."."

That was when she noticed the handmade birthday card sticking out of his pocket. She'd known it was him. The moment she saw his prized lapel pin at Tracy's house, she'd known it had to be him. But why? Evan had been more than her boss. She'd thought he was a friend.

Obviously, she was wrong.

He was going to kill her, just like he'd killed the other women. Who knew how many? Tugging back, she screamed with all her might.

Why didn't he just kill her now and get it over with? The idea renewed her energy, and she began shrieking and tugging to free herself from his hold.

"Stop screaming." He removed one hand from her

wrist and swung it at the side of her head so fast she didn't have time to duck and evade the smack.

She shrieked again, this time in agony when his palm hit her right processor. The device flew from her ear. Tears streamed unheeded down her cold cheeks as she tried to get away from the man trying to kill her. It was no use. He was so much bigger and stronger. He dragged her over to his sedan. Casually, he held her wrists with one hand and used his key fob to pop the trunk.

Her fear of small, enclosed spaces reared its head. Shaking her head, she dug her heels into the green grass, sobbing and shaking. She opened her mouth wide, needing to breathe, but she was crying too hard to get a full breath. It did no good. Inch by inch, Evan drew her alongside to the waiting, open trunk. He dropped her wrists for an instant. Before she could flee, he had swept her up in his arms and carried her as though she were a small child the remaining few feet to her fate.

He dropped her in the small, dark space. The smell of rust and mildew overwhelmed her. The fear of being trapped in a confined area washed over her, nearly smothering her and choking her before she managed to speak.

"Wait! I can't breathe in here!"

Her boss ignored her plea and barely glanced at her as he reached up and took hold of trunk. She struggled to sit, praying she could jump free before he closed her in. It was no use.

Evan slammed the trunk shut, immersing her in immediate and suffocating darkness. Already, the air was getting thin. Or was that her overactive imagination? She both hoped for him to release her soon and dreaded it. Because as much as she desperately needed out of the dark, dank, terrifying space she was enclosed in, she had no doubt that once he sprang the lock to open the trunk, her time would be up. She wasn't ready to die.

The tires struck something, most likely a pothole, and her jolt sent the metal tackle box tucked into the corner crashing into her lower back. Her entire body already ached from being folded up like a pretzel, her knees even with her hips and her neck bent at an unnatural angle. Now she could add bruises to her list of physical ailments.

Another bump sent the tackle box whizzing across the confined space to smash into the back of the trunk. The trunk shifted to the right. The car was turning. If only she could keep track of the turns. Not that it would help her. She didn't have her phone on her. And her watch battery was low, so it wouldn't be much use. Maybe the trunk had a spring. Some vehicles had a trigger of some sort one could pull, in case a child got stuck, or if one needed to open it from inside the car.

She couldn't push the seat forward and escape. Evan would kill her without a second thought.

Her only advantage was in that he hadn't tied her hands when he'd captured her. Now that she had a purpose, some of her panic faded. Feeling her way, she reached out both hands, searching for a chain or a loop. If she could find one, she'd wait until the motion of the vehicle slowed before pulling on it. Then she'd have to jump out quick.

She only hoped her legs weren't too numb to move. Her right foot, the one in contact with the bottom surface, was nearly asleep. Jostling it to reestablish blood flow, she clenched her teeth and groaned when the sensation of pins and needles darted up her leg from ankle to knee. Still, a little pain and discomfort was nothing if it meant she lived to see her daughter again. And Micah. Her heart clenched in her and it hurt to breathe. To think she might never see those she loved most again.

What would become of Shelby? She had no grandparents. No uncles or cousins. Lissa had a will— she'd made it right after her daughter's birth—and she'd named Tracy as guardian. It had never occurred to her that she would need to plan further than that.

She blew out a breath, which stirred the dust around and tickled her nose.

Micah would take care of Shelby. How she knew, she couldn't say, but in her soul the certainty that he'd see to the little girl's protection and care eclipsed all the doubt conspiring to steal her peace.

How she loved him. And he'd never know it.

Why, when she was staring death in the face, why only now did she admit to herself she loved the reticent lawman?

She had to focus. If she got out of this alive, she could tell him how felt herself.

Doubling her efforts, she scrambled inside the small space as carefully as she could. There. Was that it? She felt along the thin wire extending from the back of the truck to the round finger loop at the end. Hope burst in her chest, painful and sweet. If this worked, she'd soon be free.

Sinking down against the floor of the trunk, Lissa planted her head against the carpeted surface and, ignoring the disgusting aromas emanating from the rug, squeezed her eyes shut in an attempt to focus on the movement of the vehicle. Her head bounced with every slight hiccup.

The vibrations pulsing through her skull slowed. It was now or never. Grasping the loop, she waited until it felt like the vehicle was almost stopped, then yanked on the loop. The trunk flew open.

Triumphant, she started to sit up. Her eyes met the horrified gaze of a woman sitting in a car ten feet behind. They must be at a traffic light. That stunned moment cost her. The vehicle jerked forward, and the lid slammed down. The sudden burst of pain was the last thing she saw.

She was so cold. Shivering, she lifted her heavy lids and blinked away the confusion settled like a quilt around her. Her eyes widened. She wasn't in the trunk anymore. She was lying on a worn green futon in an overcluttered room. Scurrying to a sitting position, she took note of her surroundings. Amazed, she saw she was alone. When she attempted to stand, however, she discovered a chain stretched from her left leg to the foot of the futon. It seemed to be a home office of some sort. Or a spare bedroom. Even though her right processor was gone, her left side was still on her head and functioning. A loud, angry thumping sound reached her from another room in the house. Or was she in an apartment? Was this Evan's home? It was hard to tell. All she knew was she'd never seen this room before.

Then her glance hit the walls of the chamber. She shuddered. Bile hit the back of her throat. She swallowed hard to keep herself from vomiting. Stretching

from one end of the wall to the next, Evan had created
handmade calendars. The graphs drawn for the dates
were excruciatingly precise. It must have taken him
hours to craft them. On top in large block letters, he'd
written out the names of the months. Most of the dates
were still empty. Five of them, however, had the dates
written in.

He'd written them to correspond with the month he'd
made the kill. Five women dead. The police and the
marshals only knew about four of them. Each month
had a woman's picture on it, with a date circled. She
saw Tracy's picture glued on the April calendar, her
birthday circled in red. Her gaze skidded to a halt on
the month of May, and she did a double take. Her own
face stared out at her, smiling. Her birthdate already
circled. It was gruesome and macabre. She had no idea
how to stop it from becoming a reality. In fact, it was
hard to understand why she was still alive.

"Ah, you noted my calendars."

She'd been so horrified she had missed Evan's entrance. He surveyed the wall, pleasure etched on his
handsome face. She clasped her hands together to control the shaking. He turned his attention to her. His
smile had a hard, feral edge to it.

How had she never noticed?

"Why Evan? I thought we were friends."

He shook his head. "We were never friends, Lissa.
Although, I hadn't planned on killing you until you
found the lapel pin I'd lost before I could reclaim it."

"I don't understand. What had any of these women
done to you?" *Please Micah. Come find me.*

He stepped closer, chuckling as she shrunk away
from him. "It's not complicated. I had dated Penny

twice a few years ago. When I asked her out a third time, she refused and gave me a ridiculous line about some people shouldn't try to be more than friends. I could see she thought she was better than I was. Then she started dating that deputy marshal you've been hanging out with, and I knew I had to act."

She froze. He'd killed four women because Penny had broken up with him.

"I realized I had power," he continued. "I had a job that actually helped me plan murders. That's when the idea of a calendar would be a fitting way to track my game."

Her stomach curdled. It was a game to him. The man she thought she'd known didn't exist.

"Why Gage?"

"He suspected me. He'd come to see me to ask for time off and had gotten a look at my set up here. The door hadn't been completely closed. I had to let him get away from my house. I couldn't risk killing him here, now, could I?"

That's when she accepted she had no hope to escape on her own.

She sent up a prayer, a plea for rescue. In her heart, she knew it would be her last.

Laughing at the ridiculous jibes being tossed back and forth by Gideon and Zeke, Micah shook his head and strode along with them to the house. Lissa would get a kick out of their conversation. She was of the opinion that Zeke was rather staid and serious. But she hadn't grown up alongside him. While he appeared calm and thoughtful, he was a prankster at heart.

The memory of the morning rose up. His pulse raced.

She'd kissed him back. He had the proof he needed that she felt something for him, too. If she didn't, she would not have kissed him the second time. The first kiss had surprised both of them. He hadn't planned it. But the second one, that one had been deliberate.

"Where's my buggy?" Zeke's confused voice broke into his rumination.

"What?" He glanced around. There was no buggy in the yard. "We've been out in the workshop for two and a half hours. Iris probably put the buggy in the barn."

Zeke frowned, shaking his head. He lengthened his stride and banged through the kitchen door. Gideon and Micah glanced at each other and shrugged, then followed suit. Micah's gut clenched. His instincts were shouting something was wrong.

"Iris?" Zeke called. "*Mamm*, where's Iris?"

Micah scanned the kitchen, passing over his mother and Shelby. They were alone. In three steps, he was out of the kitchen and into the family room. No one was in there. As he rushed back to the kitchen, his gaze swerved between the others in the room. Gideon was frowning and his *mamm* was starting to look upset.

"Where's Lissa?"

He kept his voice soft. The sudden silence was unnerving.

Edith handed Shelby a cookie and told her to eat it in the kitchen. The child grabbed Sonny and the unexpected treat and dashed into the next room. The adults moved as one to the front porch. They waited until the door clanged behind them before renewing their conversation.

Edith sat at the table, her brow furrowed. "Iris asked

Micah's Lissa to come home with her and join her for some baking they'd left unfinished. I thought you two had talked about it. It sounded like a *gut* idea. I thought they were becoming friends. Iris is so shy, she needs friends."

Zeke slumped down on the bench. He didn't appear mad or worried, only perplexed. "I don't understand. She didn't mention anything about this to me. I hadn't expected her to join me this morning. She said she wanted to see you, *Mamm*."

Micah fought back the panic stirring and shaking in his belly. He forced himself to remain where he was, bracing his shoulders against the wall as if it would hold him up. His gaze darted around the room, desperate to find some clue as to what was going on. Iris was his sister-in-law. Family. Yet, every molecule in his body screamed that Lissa was in danger.

"I need to go over to your house, Zeke."

Gage was dead, Micah reminded himself. He couldn't hurt her anymore. But what if Gage wasn't the killer? What if he had been a decoy?

Without another word, he bounded out the kitchen door, ignoring his mother's voice calling him. Footsteps pounded behind him. He raced to his SUV and jumped in behind the steering wheel. Zeke yanked the passenger side open and joined him in the front seat, while Gideon hopped in the back. His mother could explain to his father where they'd gone.

The engine roared to life. He jerked the shift into Drive.

"Micah!" His *mamm* stood on the front porch, wringing her hands. Shelby stood next to her, Sonny clutched tight to her chest. The poor kid looked terrified.

He hit the button and rolled down his window. "I can't explain. No time. Please watch Shelby for me until I get back with Lissa."

He couldn't say more, not with Shelby standing there listening. The four minutes to his brother's house were the longest minutes of his life. Micah was frantic. As frantic as the day twenty-four years ago when he'd discovered his baby sister had vanished while he and his brothers were supposed to be watching her.

This couldn't be happening again.

"I'm sure everything's fine," Zeke muttered beside him in a tight voice. He swiveled his head toward his brother, a sharp retort on his tongue. The stinging remark died when he saw his brother's pale skin. Zeke's hand clutched the handle hanging from the roof, his knuckles white. Fear gleamed out of his eyes.

Their family had seen enough to trouble to know bad things happened to good people all the time.

Arriving at the house, Micah halted the vehicle beside the buggy and slammed it into Park. He didn't even bother shutting the engine off. He threw open the door and undid his seat belt simultaneously, then jumped out and ran to the door, his brothers on his heels.

Racing into the house, he yelled Lissa's name once, then stumbled to a halt.

Zeke's wife was slumped against the wall, half sitting, blood staining her white apron. Micah had seen enough bullet wounds to know she'd been shot. A trail of red made a gory path from the living room to where she sat. She'd crawled from the other room.

Zeke saw his wife's ashen complexion and blood-stained clothing and choked out her name. He fell to his knees beside her, ignoring the blood on the floor.

Micah handed Gideon his phone and ordered him to dial 911. He didn't remain to hear a response. Reaching for his weapon, he moved past the other occupants in the room, his gun in his hand, and searched the rest of the house. When he'd determined the house was clear, he returned to the kitchen. Gideon's eyes were wide, white showing around his dark irises. He'd never seen anyone shot before. He was still on the phone with 911.

Micah grabbed a clean dish towel and sank down on the other side of Iris. Her eyelids fluttered open. "Zeke. Take this and press it against her wound. Let's try and stop the blood."

It was too late, he knew it was, but his brother didn't. In years to come, he didn't want Zeke wondering what else he could have done to save his bride.

"Micah." Iris slurred. "I didn't mean for her to get hurt."

His heart stopped. Blood pounded in his ears.

"Where's Lissa?" There was no one else she could have been referring to. Was he too late? With supreme effort, he kept his voice gentle when he wanted to shout, to demand to know where Lissa was. It would do no good. Tears leaked down his brother's lean cheeks and seeped into his newly grown beard. Zeke kept his silence, though Micah knew this new agony had to be shredding him to pieces. "Iris, who took Lissa?"

Gideon gulped behind him.

"He said he'd kill my brother, Danny." She gasped, her breathing harsh and ragged. "He had him. He knew you were with Lissa, but he couldn't get close to her with all the family around. He said he'd tried. I didn't want to help him. I didn't. Had no choice. If I didn't help, Danny would die."

She had sacrificed Lissa to save her brother. The urge to yell pulsed through his throat. His muscles tightened so hard they ached.

"Who, Iris? Who has her?"

Iris's eyes closed again.

"Iris!"

Her chest heaved. A droplet of blood bubbled at the corner of her mouth. "Her boss. Evan."

Micah reeled back, falling on his heels.

Evan. It all made sense now. Evan would have as much, or more, access to the information regarding the women he targeted. He would have known Gage's habits. How long had he been planning to hand his employee to the law enforcement agencies on a platter to take the blame? It had been flawless. So perfect, in fact, that they'd dropped their guard and allowed him to take Lissa. *He'd* dropped his guard. The elation he'd felt two hours earlier fled. He'd failed her. In his overconfidence, he'd neglected to consider the idea that Gage hadn't been the mastermind behind the Birthday Card Killer.

"Iris." Zeke's groan brought his attention back to the woman on the floor. The wound had stopped bleeding, but it wasn't because of Zeke's efforts. Micah reached past his brother and felt the pulse point on her neck. There was a faint pulse still, but he knew it wouldn't be long until it stopped.

An ambulance pulled into the yard. Micah held out

his hand to Gideon, who tossed the cell phone back to him. Micah left his family and strode onto the porch, dialing Chief Spencer's number.

"Hello?"

"Chief, Micah here. We have a situation." Succinctly, he brought the chief up to speed, struggling to keep his words steady. His jaw shuddered with emotion. He squeezed his eyes shut to hold the moisture welling at bay. A tear slipped through and trickled down his face. He swiped his arm across his face.

The chief was shocked. Two minutes after they disconnected, a Be On the Look Out alert notification rang out. Micah hung his head. On his own, he had no hope of finding Lissa alive. But God could. Micah prayed, harder than he'd ever prayed in his life.

His phone rang again. His heart leaped when he saw the chief's number. "Bender here."

"Micah, we have a break." The chief spoke rapidly. "A driver on North Main Street, about eight miles from your position, had stopped at the traffic light. The trunk of the car in front of her opened, and a woman dressed in Amish clothing sat up. She looked terrified. When the car started again, the trunk closed."

Lissa. She'd been terrified, but at least they knew she was alive. There was no doubt in his mind it was his Lissa the woman had seen. She was clever enough to work through her fear of closed-in spaces and figure out how to open the trunk from the inside.

"Any idea where they were headed, Chief?"

"We're watching the cameras at the lights in real time. The car left the main roads, but it looks like he was headed back to his house. I'm sending you the address.

I have officers en route, and Deputy Marshal Gates is also on his way. We'll get her back, Micah. If it's possible, God willing, we will get her back."

Micah disconnected.

"Go."

He whirled around. He'd been so involved in the call, he hadn't heard the door open. Gideon's face was drawn and pale, anguish stamped in every line. He barely resembled the carefree younger brother Micah had been laughing with earlier. But purpose shone from his eyes.

"Take care of Zeke." No matter what Iris had done, she'd acted out of fear, not malice. And his brother loved his wife fiercely.

"You don't need to tell me that. Go save Lissa. *Gott* be with you."

Micah clapped a hand on his brother's shoulder before pivoting and leaping over the steps to the gravel driveway. He hopped into his SUV and plugged the phone into the console, tapping the address into the GPS system with trembling fingers.

The solitude enabled him to devote his full attention on the task at hand. Micah had always been a cautious driver. Growing up using buggies for travel had given him an appreciation for taking his time and seeing the beauty of the world around him, the world God had created. The current situation gave him a healthy respect for the ability to accelerate. He pressed his foot on the gas pedal, pushing the vehicle as fast as he could safely manage.

Evan's house was out in the middle of nowhere. His driveway was so long that Micah thought he'd made a wrong turn onto an unmarked dirt road. When the house appeared, he mentally thanked God. He left the car and made his way soundlessly to the side of the house. Parker was already there.

The car that had been spotted at the traffic light was at the back of the house, the trunk standing wide open.

He was there.

Sweat dampened the palms of his hands. He knew Evan was there, but still had no idea if the woman he loved was still alive. A shadow moved. Whipping his head to the left, Micah saw Lieutenant Bartlett and Steve, both with weapons drawn, advancing to the front of the house. He pointed to the right. Parker nodded, and they flattened themselves along the side of the house and edged toward the rear of the building. The rough brick exterior snagged at his jacket, scuffing the leather. They kept moving.

Suddenly, Micah paused and held up his right hand. Parker halted. They listened. Directly ahead of them, he could barely make out an angry voice through the closed window. Evan was in the house. Was Lissa with him? Peeling himself off the wall inch by inch, he peered into the room. All he could see were shadows dancing on the wall. They were indistinct, though, so he was unable to discern how many individuals were in the room. For all he knew, Evan was on the phone.

Ducking lower than the window ledge, he slid to the other side of the opening. This time when he peeked in, he saw Evan standing over the couch, shouting. Lissa cowered away from him. And from the length of rope in his hands.

He was going to strangle her.

Without thinking, Micah gave up the pretense of

skulking around to the back. With a burst of speed, he hurtled down the length of the house and crashed through the back door, his gun aloft in his hand. He charged through the house, stopping in front of a closed door. Lissa cried out. He tried the door, breathing hard. It was locked. A locked door would not stop him from saving the woman he loved. Lowering the gun, he shot the doorknob off. A loud thud echoed when the other side of the handle dropped. Shoving the door open, he raced in, leaping over the coffee table to manhandle Evan away from Lissa. The moment she was free, she dropped back on the couch, gulping in air, rubbing her throat. The red rope burn across the tender skin fueled his outrage.

He clenched his empty fist, turning to Evan. "Evan Finch, you are under arrest—"

Evan swung around, pulling a gun from the back of his pants. He aimed. Before he could fire, two gunshots split the air. He jerked, like a puppet on a string, and fell, leaving both Micah and Parker standing, their service weapons still smoking.

It was over.

He glanced at Lissa. All of it was over.

Within minutes, law enforcement, the coroner and medical personnel swarmed the scene, asking questions, declaring Evan dead and removing his body, checking on Lissa, and taking pictures. Micah's blood ran cold when he saw the calendars Evan had on the wall.

"He put my picture up before he tried to strangle me," Lissa whispered, her voice raw. He winced. The sight of the Polaroid photo of her on the May graph turned his stomach. "It's gruesome, but I think his obsession with taking the pictures gave you time. He'd forgotten his polaroid when he'd arrived at your brother's house. That's why he didn't kill me there. Had he not done that, you would have arrived too late."

Micah shuddered at her words. There was no blame, only a matter-of-fact recitation of facts. He'd been so ready to declare himself, to tell her he loved her, but now he swallowed those words. He didn't deserve her in his life. Not after he'd failed to save her. She'd saved herself. If she hadn't unlatched the trunk in the middle of town, it would have been too late when they found her.

"Stop."

He glanced down at her beloved, exhausted face. "Micah, this is not your fault."

He shrugged, unable to believe her words.

She took his hand in both of hers. "I promised myself, if I survived, I would be done protecting myself from life. I would embrace what God has given me."

His heart was lead in his chest. He knew where this was headed. He placed a finger over her lips to quiet her. "Lissa, don't say it. I don't deserve your love. I failed you. Spectacularly."

"No." She shook her head, her brown hair swinging in waves over her shoulders. "You didn't. It was all him."

He couldn't take it. His soul was shattered. It might never be whole again. "I can't. I need time. I'm too broken. You need someone whole."

"I need you. I love you, Micah."

There it was.

"I love you, too. But I have nothing to give you. Not now. I need to figure this out. I can't keep adding one burden on top of another. Joss. Penny. Now you and Shelby. I have to find a way to make peace with myself."

His vision blurred. Before she could protest, he left the room. He'd make plans for Parker or someone else to return Lissa and Shelby home. Then he'd try to deal with the emptiness that had become his life.

SEVENTEEN

Steve's Ford F-150 pickup truck was parked near the front barn when Micah arrived at his parents' house. Micah parked behind it, giving the vehicle enough room so Joss and Steve could make a quick getaway if needed. One never knew what might happen when a four-month-old baby was involved. Or a new father. He smirked. Joss had handled motherhood with ease, no doubt because working in a pediatrician's office for several years had clued her in to what was on the horizon. Steve, though, tended to get more anxious with every new development.

Shaking his head, Micah hefted the large watermelon he'd brought and left his vehicle. Following the sound of voices, he strolled toward the main house. The mid-morning sun warmed the top of his head. It was already seventy-four degrees in the shade. It would hit close to eighty today, with no chance of rain. The perfect day for a picnic.

He sighed in relief when he heard Zeke's quiet voice. After Iris died two months ago, Zeke had refused to live in the house where her blood had stained the floor. He'd

called the local volunteer fire department and told them
to use it as a training exercise for their members, several of whom were Amish. Then he'd left without telling anyone where he'd gone. They'd all been afraid he'd
disappear like Isaiah had. But Zeke had returned three
weeks ago, quieter than ever, but at least he was back.

Beyond the main house, he saw shadows moving
around the smaller house on the property. It was nearly
finished. He'd been building the *dawdi haus* with his
daed and his two brothers. Steve had even stepped in
and lent a hand, even though he wasn't Amish. Micah's
daed had started talking about moving to the *dawdi
haus* when Zeke moved into his own home and Gideon
married, assuming the youngest son ever found a wife.
In Amish tradition, the youngest child inherited the
house and the parents would downsize into a smaller
home on the property. That might be years away, still,
but it was always best to be prepared.

Micah sighed. The community had banded together
and rebuilt Zeke's house, helping out a neighbor in need,
as was their tradition. Still, Zeke hadn't spent more than
a handful of nights in the new place.

"It doesn't make sense, living there all alone with
Iris gone," he'd confessed to Micah. "Even though it's
not the same *haus*, Iris and I bought that land together.
It feels wrong."

Micah had nodded. Yeah, he knew about things
not making sense. He hadn't seen Lissa, or Shelby, for
nearly two months. His heart grew heavier in his chest
each morning when he arose and thought about the day
ahead. He filled it with work and fixing things around
his house.

But it was an empty existence. Only his faith kept him focused and moving forward. He'd been tempted to stay home instead of joining his family at the family dinner. Why force his bad mood on everyone else? However, no matter how dark his world seemed without a certain brunette and her sweet, spunky daughter, he wouldn't hurt his *mamm* by distancing himself from the family. He'd done that when he left years ago, and he could see how Isaiah's absence was like a yawning hole in his parents' hearts.

Laughter interrupted his morose musings. His head swung to the left in time to see Steve give Joss a gentle push on the tire swing attached to a thick branch on the old maple tree. That swing had been there as long as he could remember. The rope was new, though. His *daed* must have replaced it for the next generation.

The swing swung back and Steve caught it, leaning down to give his wife a tender kiss before releasing it. The greeting died on his lips. He watched as the scene replayed.

He could picture himself and Lissa there. And Shelby... That sweet little girl would love that swing.

He cleared his throat and called out a greeting, shoving thoughts of Lissa and Shelby to the side. But never out of mind. No matter where he went, they were always with him. He longed to return to Lissa and claim the love she'd offered, but the longer he stayed away, the more unworthy of her he felt.

"Micah!" Joss stopped the swing with her feet and let her husband assist her out of it. She rewarded him with a light kiss on the cheek before skipping over to where her oldest brother stood. Micah knew what was coming. He held out his arms as she launched herself at him, squeezing tight. He closed his eyes, thanking God for returning his sister to his life. Joss loved all her brothers, although she'd never met Isaiah before, but she and Micah shared a special relationship. Maybe because he'd been the first person in the family she'd met, or possibly because he'd been deeply involved in solving her abduction case and bringing the criminals to justice. Whatever the reason, Micah was thankful to have her back.

"Hey, sis. I thought you were an adult now."

She laughed and hugged for two more seconds before stepping back, pushing her brown hair behind her ears. "Just because I'm a parent now, doesn't mean I've forgotten how to enjoy the simple things in life."

Her gaze roamed his face, worry lurking behind the smile.

He broke her gaze and focused on his brother-in-law. "Glad you were able to get the day off. The last I heard, you were supposed to be out of town to testify at a trial."

Steve sauntered close and draped an affectionate arm around his wife. "You remember right. The trial date got postponed. So, you're stuck with me for the day."

Chatting together, mostly about the new and wonderful things baby Christina was doing on a daily basis, they meandered into the house. Micah greeted his mother with a kiss on her cheek and handed her the watermelon he'd picked up on the way there.

"*Ack, danke*. This will be perfect for after the main meal. You *kinder* can eat it on the picnic table and throw the rinds in the field. *Gut* fertilizer, ain't so?"

Micah chuckled. He was thirty-two, and Joss was a

wife with a child of her own, but in his parents' sight, they were all still children.

"Yes, *Mamm*." He and Joss murmured together, shooting each other grins. A small cry began in the other room. Joss disappeared briefly, returning with the cutest little four-month-old baby, in his opinion. Immediately, his mother's attention was diverted to her only grandchild.

"Hmm. Off with you now. Your father is over at the *dawdi haus*. You boys should go assist him and your brothers."

"And just like that, we're forgotten."

Steve laughed. Together they drifted across the lush green lawn to the new *dawdi haus*.

Micah's *daed* broke off what he'd been telling Zeke. "Micah. Steve. *Cumme*. Join us. There's much to do before we eat."

Zeke nodded his own quiet welcome.

Gideon, however, scowled at Micah. Taken aback, Micah stopped in his tracks. Gideon stomped over to him and jerked his head, motioning for Micah to come with him. "We'll be back."

Stunned by his brother's almost angry manner, Micah went with him. Gideon was never mad. Nor did he stomp or growl, not like he was doing now. Whatever had happened, it must have been serious.

They walked nearly to the main barn before Gideon halted next to Micah's vehicle. Micah's eyebrows rose when the younger man faced him, muscular arms folded across his chest.

"Okay, Gideon, you're starting to concern me. This isn't like you."

Gideon narrowed his bright blue eyes. "Well, I had always thought you were smart, *ja*? But now I'm beginning to think maybe you're not so wonderful clever, you know?"

All right. Something was definitely wrong, but he still didn't understand what. "Gid, what's bothering you? Seriously, I have no idea what this is about."

Gideon threw his hands up. "It's about how I have two brothers moping around like their hearts are broken. Zeke, I understand. *Ja*, his *frau* is dead. And she betrayed him before she died. But you?" He took a step closer, narrowing his eyes. "Why isn't Lissa here with you? It's clear you love her."

Micah blinked. He opened his mouth to answer, but no words came out. The last thing he'd expected when he arrived was for his cheerful and carefree brother to all but attack him for not bringing Lissa to the family picnic.

"Well?"

Rubbing the back of his neck, Micah tried to put his chaotic thoughts into words. "It's not that easy, Gid. I had some stuff I had to work through."

"Guilt." Gideon all but spat. "As if you had anything to do with Penny's death. Or with Joss's kidnapping. Or even with Lissa's problems. Only *Gott* can control events of that nature. We do the best we can to handle what comes our way and trust Him."

He stared. "When you put it that way, it sounds—"

"Conceited?"

That startled a laugh out of him. "I guess, although not the word I would have used." Micah sighed. "I have been very confused, and I guess the longer I took to figure out my mind, the less certain I was that she'd welcome me back. It's been two months, Gideon. What if she decided I'm not worth it?"

Gideon snorted. "What if she didn't? You'll never know if you don't go to her and find out."

Micah shoved his hands in the pockets of his jeans, thinking. "Okay, so tomorrow—"

"*Nee.* Not tomorrow. That leaves room for more excuses. I will talk to *mamm.* We can hold eating off until you get back. It's only going on ten thirty. If you go to her now, you can be back by one, don't ya think?"

Hope bloomed in his chest and began to spread through his blood. He could do this. What did he have to lose? He was already living a life without his girls. "I could do that. If she doesn't slam the door in my face."

He'd totally deserve it if she did.

"You have to try. When you *cumme* back, I hope to see my future sister-in-law and niece with you."

Micah grabbed his brother in a rare hug, pounded on his back a couple of times and received a couple of poundings on his own back. Then he jumped into his SUV before he could talk himself out of it. Gideon took off at a run to the house.

It would take him forty-five minutes to reach Lissa's house. He'd use every minute of the drive there to pray for guidance and wisdom.

It was time to go see Lissa and plead for forgiveness.

Lissa clipped the last of Shelby's shirts to the clothesline. A warm breeze ruffled the fabric, lifting her ponytail off her neck. She closed her eyes and raised her face, enjoying the warmth on her cheeks.

Would today be the day?

She crushed the thought before it had fully formed. She'd hoped, for two long months, that Micah would text, or call. Just some sort of communication to let her know he was healthy and that he was thinking of her. Nothing. Her shattered heart couldn't take any more broken hopes.

Shelby, with the resilience of youth, didn't have the same misgivings. She was determined that Marshal Micah would come back each day. After all, he'd said he'd return when he could. Her young heart hadn't learned that sometimes adults said one thing and did another. Lissa hadn't thought Micah would be one of those people who'd disappoint a child, but the current situation forced her to accept her judgment might have been off.

"Mama! Mama!" The back door banged shut.

Lissa heard a thud. She knew that sound. Shelby had taken a flying leap off the back porch, despite being told not to.

"One of these days you're going to drop Sonny in the dirt when you do that, Shelby," Lissa scolded her daughter. She picked up the laundry basket and moved to return to the house.

Shelby stood before her, a mile-wide grin on her face, Sonny in her arms. Directly behind the child, Micah stood, hands in his pocket, blue eyes glued to Lissa's face.

"Micah." That was all she could get out before her throat closed. So many nights, his face filled her dreams. During quiet moments, his smile swam around in her restless mind. As time passed, she'd thought of what she'd say when he returned. If he returned. Sometimes the speeches she composed were angry, sometimes sad.

Now that the moment was upon her, all her previous thoughts and ideas of what she'd say to him fled, leaving her speechless.

He was here.

"Shelby, Sweet Pea, go inside, please? You can watch your pony movie." Shelby dashed into the house.

The two adults stared at each, silently. She waited for him to break the silence. He shifted his stance. That was when she realized her big, confident man was nervous. Seeing him unsettled was not pleasant.

Finally, he took one step closer. Then a second, bringing him within arms' reach.

"Lissa."

"You never called." Really? That was the first thing she said. She shook her head and took a deep breath to slow the thoughts careening inside of her brain. "What happened, Micah? You said you needed to figure things out, but you'd be back. That was seven weeks ago. You never contacted me. I figured you'd decided we had no future."

Some of the color bled from his face. "No! I didn't decide that, not at all."

"Explain it to me, then. Why didn't you come back sooner?"

He began to pace in front of her. Only for a minute, though. Even in his distress, he remained considerate of her needs and made sure to stop so she could see his face while he talked. The protective shell she'd built around her heart cracked. "I didn't want to stay away. I know I haven't shown it very well, but I wanted to come back. To have you and Shelby in my life. It might sound like an excuse, but I always feared that I'd let you down. Which is ironic, because in staying gone, that's exactly what I did."

She shook her head. "Back up. How exactly did you think you'd let us down?"

He shrugged, ducking his head. "I don't have a good record for keeping those I love safe."

"That's one of the most absurd things I've ever heard."

His head jerked up at that. His mouth dropped open.

"Oh, I know what you thought. Micah, you were eight when your sister was kidnapped. And it was Evan who killed your fiancée. If I recall my facts, she was the first one he killed. How were you supposed to guard against that?" She placed her hands on his cheeks, cradled his beloved face. "You saved me and Shelby when no one else could. You are a good man, a praying man. You are kind to your family, trusted by your colleagues. And you are loved, so loved. Shelby adores you. So do I."

Had she said too much?

His eyes misted. He placed his hands over hers and removed them from his face. He slowly kissed her left hand, then her right one, before holding them to his chest. Her pulse shifted into overdrive. She could feel the steady beat of his own heart under her palms.

"I can't believe it's only been two months since I saw you. It feels like a lifetime. I have thought about you every hour of every day, Lissa. I told you I loved you before I left, and I do. My life has been so empty without you and Shelby."

She leaned her head against his shoulder, fighting a

losing battle with the tears that welled up. Surrendering, she closed her lids and let them fall. Micah placed a gentle hand under her chin and lifted her face to his. He kissed away the tears on her cheeks.

"I bought this weeks ago."

Her gaze snapped to his hand. She gasped. In his palm, a diamond and pearl engagement ring sparkled.

"Micah," she breathed, barely able to hear her own voice over the blood thrumming in her ears.

"Will you marry me, Lissa?"

"Yes," she choked.

He slid the ring on her finger. It was a perfect fit. "If you don't like this one…"

"It's perfect."

They smiled mistily at each other. She couldn't help herself. Reaching out, she touched his shoulder again, just to assure herself he was real.

He grinned crookedly. "One thing, though. I might have promised Gideon I'd be bringing you and Shelby back to my parents' house for our family get together."

She caught her breath. "Would it be okay? I mean, with Zeke?"

He seemed to understand. "Zeke doesn't blame you for Iris's choices. My whole family would love it if you joined us. But I understand if you have other plans."

"What could be more important than joining my future husband and his family?"

Shelby was over the moon when she learned she'd see Micah's mama again.

The rest of the day was a blur. Micah and Lissa gathered a thrilled Shelby and loaded up into his SUV. The journey to his parents' house was filled with laughter. Lissa couldn't wipe the smile from her face. Joy surged through her every time she cast her glance at the man sitting beside her. Her fiancé. She thanked God for returning him to them.

Micah executed a smooth turn onto his parents' road, then slid his hand under hers on the center armrest, twining their fingers together. He'd done that several times now, as if he couldn't bear to be apart from her even though they were in the same car. She didn't mind. Each touch sent shivers of happiness and anticipation zinging through her. She'd have a lifetime of such simple delights.

At the Bender farm, Micah parked his car behind a pickup truck, then jumped out and ran around the front of the SUV to open the door for his "girls". Lissa grinned. She loved that she and Shelby had a place in his life, at last.

The front door of the house burst open. The entire Bender family tramped onto the porch, carrying plates and dishes. Grinning, Micah held out a hand to Shelby. The little girl grasped his hand. He reached his free hand to Lissa. She saw Gideon wink at his brother. He'd told her about his younger brother giving him the business about her. She'd thank her future brother when she had the chance.

They approached his family as a unit. Micah's parents and siblings welcomed her and Shelby with open arms. His mother hugged Shelby, and Gideon enticed squeals and giggles from her with a friendly tickle.

The meal was a happy event, for the most part. Shelby and Christina were a large part of the focus. Gideon kept them laughing. Even Zeke managed to smile a time or two, despite the fact he was still mourning his wife. Lissa had worried her presence would be painful to Zeke. After the meal, he found a moment to seek her out in private.

"I saw you watching me at the table," he said simply.

Micah rounded the side of the house, pausing when he saw his brother and Lissa standing together. She shook her head. He tilted his head, considering, then gave her a thumbs-up before vanishing again.

"I was afraid it would be too much, seeing me again."

"Lissa, my wife made a bad choice. But that wasn't your fault. You are not responsible for her choices."

She recalled Micah saying something similar several hours earlier.

"She didn't act with malice."

"*Ack*. I know this. Don't fret about me."

She had to accept that he was speaking the truth. The pain had etched new lines on his face, but she had done all she could.

Later, after she and Micah were back at her house and Shelby was in bed, she relayed the conversation with him.

He was silent for a full minute. "Gideon said she'd betrayed her husband, but maybe it wasn't a betrayal so much as poor judgment. I can't hold that against her. Not when my own poor judgment nearly cost me the woman I love."

She put her arms around his neck and tried to infuse all the love she felt into her gaze. "You didn't lose me. And you won't. I will love you, Micah Bender, until the day I die."

He smiled and leaned closer. Her lids fluttered shut as their lips met, sealing the promise.

EPILOGUE

Micah set his suitcase down in the hallway right inside the front door, then stretched his arms out. The three-hour flight, squeezed into airplane seats that didn't leave enough room for his legs to fully extend, had been followed by an hour-long drive from the airport. The traffic in Columbus had been stop-and-go. He could have planned to take a later flight. But that would have meant arriving home past ten at night.

"Daddy!" His number one reason for sacrificing his personal comfort so he could be home before bedtime zoomed around the corner and flung herself into his arms.

Laughing, exhaustion forgotten, he swung her up in his arms. "Well, hello, Shelby Lu. How are you?"

She giggled at his pet name for her. "Daddy, I'm too old to swing like a baby. I'm going to start first grade tomorrow."

"No!" He pretended to drop her, catching her at the last moment. She squealed and laughed again. "Surely not. You can't be getting so grown-up. Where's Mama?"

If her implants were in, she had to have heard them. Shelby and he were making quite a racket in the hall.

"In the kitchen," Shelby responded. "She said I should have some Daddy time."

Micah grinned. His wife understood him well. He now understood why men said they had a special bond with their daughters. There was nothing in the world like being a father. Every day, he prayed for guidance to help him be the best husband and father he possibly could be.

"Let's go find her." He held his adopted daughter's hand, and they made their way through the spacious living to the kitchen. When they'd found the house, the color scheme had been hideous. Lissa, however, had immediately seen the potential. It took the first six months of their marriage to get the house the way she wanted it, but he had to admit, she'd taken it and made the old house into a home.

She'd also made a break from the career that had brought her so much pain. With Micah's support, Lissa had turned her back on anything to do with law enforcement and had opened an online baking and catering business. It had been slow going at first, but the women in his parents' district had willingly whipped up an assortment of baked goods for her to sell to ramp up her inventory until she was established. Her business really started to take off, however, in June when she was hired to cater five weddings in two months. Joss and his mother had both helped and the events were a success. In fact, they were so successful that Joss was now working with Lissa part-time.

Her energy was one of the most amazing characteristics. That, and the love and joy she and her daughter had brought into his life.

He didn't ever want to go back to how life was without them.

Lissa glanced up as they entered the kitchen. A smile burst free when she saw him. "Micah! I heard you come in."

How could she have missed it?

"I figured. Our girl said you were giving us some daddy-daughter time." Marching across the room, he met her as she rose from her chair and swooped her into his arms, kissing her softly with all the love in his heart. Behind them, Shelby made gagging noises. He smiled against his wife's lips.

Lissa settled into his embrace, her head against his shoulder and her arms winding around his waist. Together, they half turned to face Shelby. Lissa grinned at Shelby. "Do you have a problem with your parents kissing?"

The child made a face. "Mama, I don't want to talk about kissing. I want tacos!"

"Tacos it is." Lissa reached up and planted one last kiss on Micah's lips before slipping from his arms and padding over to the meat simmering on the stove in her bare feet. She sprinkled in some seasoning.

Micah watched her stir the mixture for a moment, contentment filling his soul.

"Dinner will be ready in five minutes."

"You hear that?" Micah said to Shelby. "Let's wash up and help Mama set the table."

There was no feeling that equaled the joy of sitting down to a meal with his family after being away for two days. Two long, exhausting days.

After the dishes had been done, they played a board game. Then it was time for Shelby to go to bed. She picked the story she wanted him to read, but yawned before he even finished the first page. By the time he'd read three, she was sound asleep. He stooped and kissed her forehead.

He found Lissa in the kitchen, scooping out two small bowls of ice cream. Opening the refrigerator, he pulled out the jar of hot fudge, plopped a small amount in a glass dish, and put it in the microwave. When the appliance dinged, he removed the decadent topping. Lissa smiled and winked before pouring the hot fudge over both mounds of vanilla bean ice cream.

Taking their treats to the back deck, they sat together on the Amish-made glider chair. His father had made it for them as a wedding gift. It was just big enough for two people to sit together on a warm night.

"Mmm. That was so good." Lissa licked the rest of the chocolate off her spoon.

Micah held out his hand for her dish. When she handed it to him, he placed both empty bowls on the small square table next to him and draped his arm across his wife's shoulders. They sat in silence for a few moments, enjoying the gentle motion of the glider and the fresh breeze. It brought the scent of lilacs.

"I can smell your lilac bushes."

She sniffed luxuriously. "I love that smell."

"Me, too." He shifted gears. "I can't believe Shelby will be in first grade."

"I know. It seems strange, doesn't it? Sixteen months ago, we were practically strangers."

He nodded. "It amazes me that we've only been married nine months. It feels like we've always been together."

"I know. Hey, Zeke stopped by to see you while you

were out of town. He was in the neighborhood, or so he said."

"Oh yeah? How did he seem to you?" They'd both worried about Zeke. He'd shut himself off for a while and was only now starting to rejoin in family gatherings.

"Really quiet. And that's saying something, considering its Zeke."

He shook his head. He'd need to continue to hold his brother up in prayer, but then, he prayed for all his siblings daily.

"Oh!" Lissa stopped the glider's motion with her feet and leaned forward, both hands pressing on her stomach.

"Lissa?" Alarmed, he scooted closer.

"Shush. Wait a moment." Her eyes closed and her brow furrowed in concentration. He held his breath. Suddenly, her lids popped open. "There it is!"

Turning to him, she grinned, tears in her eyes. "He moved."

Overwhelmed, Micah placed his palm over her hand. He had no words. They'd both started to worry because she hadn't felt any movement yet and had gone to get an ultrasound done two weeks ago. The technician had showed them their little boy, gently moving in her womb.

"He's like Zeke," Micah choked out. "Quiet and contemplative."

Lissa burrowed her head into his shoulder. "I'm so happy. I wish we could tell your family."

He nodded. His parents were pretty old-school. Pregnancy wasn't something openly discussed, not even among family. "Let's call Joss and Steve. They'll be thrilled."

He'd barely finished the sentence when she jumped up and grabbed her phone from her back pocket. He stood. She held it for a moment, met his eyes, then slid the phone back and settled into his arms again.

He looped both arms around her and held on tight. "I thought you wanted to call?"

She leaned away from him and wrapped her arms around his neck, burying her fingers into his hair. "I do. And I will call. But for the moment, I want to enjoy this moment with my husband. Everyone else will know soon enough."

Love for her swelled inside him. Dipping his head, he brushed her lips with his before kissing her, deeply. He'd vowed to love, honor and cherish. He intended to do just that.

* * * * *

Dear Reader,

I have always loved book series that take a secondary character and give them their own story. It's so much fun seeing how characters grow and change through several books. I am blessed that with Love Inspired Suspense, I am able to do just that, even though each book can be read by itself.

I introduced Micah in Her Secret Amish Past. He intrigued me, the formerly Amish deputy US marshal. I wanted to give him a story that showcased his strength and dedication.

Lissa is a new character. She works as a crime scene cleaner to provide for her adorable daughter. This puts her and everything she loves at risk and she needs to learn to trust others. Trust has been a common theme in my books.

I love to hear from readers. Sign up for my newsletter or contact me at www.danarlynn.com.

Blessings,
Dana R. Lynn

Get 4 FREE REWARDS!

We'll send you 2 FREE Books plus 2 FREE Mystery Gifts.

Both the *Love Inspired*® and *Love Inspired*® Suspense series feature compelling novels filled with inspirational romance, faith, forgiveness and hope.

HARLEQUIN
PLUS

Try the best multimedia subscription service for romance readers like you!

Read, Watch and Play.

Experience the easiest way to get the romance content you crave.

Start your **FREE TRIAL** at
www.harlequinplus.com/freetrial.